SHARP SHOOTIN' JUSTICE

The outlaw's cabin was barely visible down in the draw.

Up on higher gro [illegible] Gideon Magee had his [illegible] ailed the three m [illegible] thieves [illegible] he Chero-kee N [illegible] efore they headed [illegible]

Sudd [illegible]. The abin door [illegible] Gideon ould have s [illegible] his sigh s be-fore he [illegible]

And [illegible] s sadd e. It look [illegible] re a [illegible] to m ke a run [illegible] is carbine [illegible] lder, took carefu im.

The rst sho [illegible] the other [illegible] his h The hardc [illegible] nd [illegible] ped on [illegible] ack.

I [illegible] k Ma [illegible] bullet [illegible] knock hi [illegible] f his ho [illegible] rol [illegible] to a nearby ocky cre [illegible] s b [illegible] nning [illegible] int [illegible] wa-ter.

[illegible] loaded his ri-fle.

He had one more man to kill.

DEATH ON THE TEXAS RANGE

PATRICK E. ANDREWS

ZEBRA BOOKS
KENSINGTON PUBLISHING CORP.

This book is dedicated to my cousin

D.B.BURNS

of Hobart, Oklahoma

ZEBRA BOOKS

are published by

Kensington Publishing Corp.
475 Park Avenue South
New York, NY 10016

First printing: July, 1992

Printed in the United States of America

Prologue

The slim, hard-looking man stepped through the door of Dallas's Windsor Hotel and walked in a few paces before coming to a stop. For a few moments his steel-blue eyes surveyed the scene before him, as was always his habit when first entering a place. He could see only a few casual loungers and hangers-on scattered among the establishment's plush chairs and sofas.

After a moment he walked toward the registration desk in slow, long strides. His long coat covered a holstered six-shooter, and from the way his hand danced over the iron it was easy to tell he was ready to use it in an instant.

The well-cut suit he wore was a good fit, but it appeared to have been recently pulled from the bottom of a valise, which was exactly the case. He wore a derby hat that was not exactly new but showed very little use. He didn't seem at all comfortable with the headgear. In fact, he was used to the wider brim and higher crown an outdoorsman would wear.

The clerk looked up at the man's approach. "Yes, sir. And how may I help you today?"

The voice was deep but with a soft quality. "I'm supposed to meet Mr. Pascal Bond here. I was told to check in here at the desk."

"Just a moment, sir." The clerk brought out a sheaf of papers from behind the desk. He deftly went through them until he found what he was looking for. "Would you be Captain Delano, sir?"

"That's me," Charlie Delano answered. Then he added, "Texas Ranger."

"You'll find Mr. Bond in room four on the first landing, Captain," the clerk said. "Go up the stairs there and turn left. He's expecting you."

"Thank you," Charlie said.

Charlie once more carefully surveyed the lobby as he walked slowly to the stairs. He went up to the landing, and following the clerk's directions, he went to the left until he found a door with the number he was looking for. He knocked.

"Yes?"

"Cap'n Delano," he said, announcing himself.

The door opened, and a short, balding man stood there with a look of anticipation on his face. "Ah, Captain Delano. I am Pascal Bond. Please come in, sir."

Charlie merely nodded his thanks and stepped inside. The room wasn't for staying overnight. It was a small conference area set up for quick meetings between businessmen or others who required a quiet place to hold a session out of sight and earshot of any possible eavesdroppers. It could be a handy place no matter what side of the law the chamber's users were on.

"I've had some coffee brought up," Bond said. "And I've been told you have a fondness for bourbon."

"Kentucky bourbon," Charlie said.

"Then Kentucky it is, Captain. Over there on the table. Help yourself."

Charlie found a tumbler and poured himself a generous glassful. Then he walked over to a chair and sat down. He remained silent, looking only at his host.

Bond cleared his throat. "Captain Delano, I'm on Governor Coke's staff. My main job is to act as liaison between the governor's office and General William Steele."

Charlie sipped his bourbon and again nodded.

"I believe you are not presently assigned to the Frontier Battalion and that you report directly to the general, do you not?" Bond asked.

"Yes."

Bond pulled a letter from his inside coat pocket and handed it over. "I have been instructed to deliver this to you. It is a special authorization from General Steele for you to go on a very unusual sort of assignment."

Charlie took the missive and carefully read it. "He's giving me a choice on whether to accept the job or not."

"That, Captain Delano, was the governor's idea," Bond said. "After I've explained the situation, then you can decide. Believe me, sir, your reputation is well-known and respected in the highest circles of the state government. If you refuse, we'll understand and there'll be no hard feelings. And, of course, no less respect for you."

Charlie treated himself to another swallow of bourbon. "Then I reckon, you'd best get on with it, Mr. Bond."

"You know of Ace Erickson, do you not?"

"Sure," Charlie said. "He's got the town o' Stavanger wrapped up in a pretty package and tied with a bright red ribbon. It's a present he's give hisself."

"You're absolutely correct about that, Captain," Bond said. "He's the mastermind behind the biggest bank and train robberies in the state of Texas. And we've done our best to bring him to justice."

"He's tricky, ain't he?" Charlie remarked. He finished the drink and got up to make another.

"Erickson runs his outlaw empire with three elements, Captain," Bond explained. "A gang of hired guns, a self-appointed lawman, and a smooth-talking, oily lawyer by the name of Maxwell Banter."

Charlie came back and sat down. "I believe that lawman is the Stavanger town sheriff. Name o' Gustavo Fairweather."

"Correct, Captain," Bond said. "I'm please you've developed this information. I presume you know Gustavo Fairweather."

Charlie cracked a quick grin. "We've bumped heads now and then."

"Well, Captain, nothing we've been able to do has brought those three to justice. Warrants, investigations, and other maneuverings inside the law have all been foiled by Erickson and Banter through bribes, threats, and influence-peddling."

Charlie once more grinned slightly. "I notice you said, *inside* the law."

"I think you're getting my drift, Captain Delano," Bond said.

"Go on, Mr. Bond."

"We want you to go after Erickson any way you can," Bond said. "And that means inside as well as *outside* the law. But you won't get any open, official backing, since a heavy political backlash is possible under those circumstances. We are talking about base crime carried on in a most sophisticated manner."

"You folks seem to be in a hurry to get this case under way," Charlie said.

"You're right," Bond said. "The reason being that it won't be too long before Erickson and Banter maneuver a man of theirs into the Texas legislature. If that happens, we'll never get rid of them."

"How come I'm being brung in on this?" Charlie asked.

"You've got a reputation of being an experienced outlaw fighter who knows how to keep your mouth shut when you bend the law to your own benefit. And it is well known in certain law-enforcement circles that you have a talent for creating chaos in order to establish the peace. A very unusual and useful talent in these times." Bond walked to another chair and sat down. "How long do you need to decide?"

"I've already decided," Charlie said. "I'll take the job."

Bond smiled. "We figured you would."

Charlie said, "From what I know about Erickson, I won't be able to do much to him in Stavanger. The real fight is going to be out in the open country."

"That is exactly the opinion that General Steele has expressed, Captain," Bond said. "Therefore, it must be a correct assumption."

"This here authorization from General Steele lets me recruit men into the Rangers. I'd rather get new ones than drag in any other fellers already in the force that I know. Most of 'em got long service, and if things go wrong, it could ruin their careers."

"That's fine," Bond said. "I presume you know some qualified people. How many are you going to get to help you?"

"Two," Charlie answered.

"Two! Only two?"

"If you knowed that pair of son of a bitches like I did, you'd know they'd be enough," Charlie said. He finished his drink and stood up.

"I'll trust your judgment on that, Captain, and so will the governor," Bond said. "We would like you to keep in touch by telegraph whenever possible. I can be reached here at the Windsor Hotel. Anytime they receive a wire in my name, they will dispatch it to the proper office."

"Fine," Charlie said. "I'm on my way."

"You're ready to leave this quick?" Bond asked.

"I reckon. So long, Mr. Bond."

"Good-bye, Captain Delano. You've taken on a difficult and very dangerous assignment, sir," Bond said in open admiration and respect. "I wish the best of luck to you."

Charlie went to the door and turned around. "There might not be enough luck in the whole world for this go-round. So long, Mr. Bond."

One

Guy Tyrone, deputy sheriff of Sweetwater, Texas, stepped out of the Texas Star Cafe and walked to the edge of the boardwalk. He stood there for a while, absentmindedly staring at the busy scene in the street while working the toothpick in his mouth. It was a warm, pleasant afternoon, the kind that made him glad he didn't have a regular job to work at. It was nice not to have a whole lot to do.

Guy enjoyed the memory of the large hunk of apple pie he'd just finished. The young waitress in the place liked him. He didn't think she was particularly pretty, but he was always nice to the girl and flirted a little to make her think he was kind of sweet on her. That way she always gave him extra big helpings of whatever he ordered. A rail-thin twenty-three-year-old, Guy could put away food like a starving lumberjack without gaining a pound of weight. He was tall and slightly stoop-shouldered with the strength and flexibility of a bullwhip in his long arms.

"Deputy Tyrone!"

Guy looked to see an excited man, waving and gesturing, hurrying his way. He turned and walked toward the fellow, hoping that something with a lot of busy and bother was not in the offing. "Howdy, Mr. Duncan."

"Howdy," Duncan said. He was a grizzled farmer who had a small place just outside town. Do you recollect them cows that was stole from me last week?"

"Sure do," Guy replied.

"Well, Ned Turnbull just tole me he seen 'em both over at a feedlot in Mitchell County. And he knows the name o' the feller that's got 'em in hand. That don't mean he stole 'em, but it means he's gotta give them critters back, right?"

"You got 'em branded or ear-notched?" Guy asked.

"I got 'em notched and the pattern is in the county courthouse," Duncan said.

"The law is on your side, Mr. Duncan," Guy said. "As soon as the sheriff gets back into town, I'll tell him about it. He'll go over and fetch 'em for you. And if he gets a lead on who took the cows over there, he'll arrest him and bring him back here for trial."

Duncan frowned. "Why the hell do you gotta wait for the sheriff? Go on over there and get 'em yourself."

Guy shook his head. "Hell, I can't go over to Mitchell County. The law'll arrest me."

"Aw, damn! Are you wanted over there?"

"Sure enough," Guy said. "They got a coupla warrants on me for disturbing the peace. I sure as hell ain't going over and have the sheriff throw me in jail."

"Tell the law you're on official duty."

"Won't do no good," Guy said. "The Mitchell County sheriff has got it in for me."

"Damn, Deputy Tyrone!" Duncan exclaimed in exasperation.

"Sorry, Mr. Duncan," Guy said. "If them cows was in Fisher or Coke County, I'd—" He hesitated. "If they was in Fisher County anyhow, I'd run over and get 'em for you."

"Aw, damn, Deputy Tyrone!" Duncan wailed again.

Guy shrugged. "So you see, even if I went over there, I couldn't get 'em back anyhow. Don't worry. You'll get 'em by day after tomorrow at the latest."

"I reckon it can't be helped," Duncan said. He gave a dispirited wave and walked away.

Guy went on down the street toward the jail, his left hand idly tapping the fourteen-inch billy club he carried looped over a special hook on his belt.

The young deputy was well-liked in Sweetwater, and replied to the friendly greetings from folks as he slowly walked along the row of stores and other businesses. When he passed the Good Time Saloon, he peered inside. He noted a lone, armed man standing at the bar, quietly drinking. The fellow was a stranger in town and had the look of just coming in off the trail. Guy turned in and walked through the batwing doors. He went directly to the drinker.

"Howdy," the deputy sheriff said.

The man looked at him. "Howdy." He noted the star on the other's vest, then turned his attention back to his drink.

"We got a city ordinance that don't allow no gun-packing," Guy said. "Unless you're just passing through."

"I'm just passing through," the man said.

"No you ain't," Guy pointed out. "You're standing at the bar here drinking whiskey."

"Well, then, I'll be passing through directly," the man said.

"Meanwhile, I'll take your iron," Guy said. "Gimme it."

"Go to hell, Slim," the man replied.

"Want to see something?" Guy asked.

The man turned again. "Sure."

Guy reached down and pulled the billy club off its hook. It was a round, well-sanded stick of dark wood. "Do you know what this is?"

"Looks like one o' them billy clubs or something," the drinker said.

"It's something like that," Guy said. "It's made outta wood from South America—called jirara wood. That's the hardest wood knowed to man.

"Is that right?"

"I don't know. You tell me." Guy hit the man hard along the side of the head, sending him stumbling so bad he fell to the floor.

The stranger rolled over on the floor and sat up. He rubbed his head, then got slowly to his feet. "Goddamn, Slim!"

"You'll call me deputy," Guy said in a calm voice.

"Goddamn, Deputy!"

"Now undo that gunbelt and drop it."

The man complied, letting the weapon hit the floor. "Can I get up and go back to drinking my whiskey?"

"Sure," Guy replied. He waited for the fellow to go back to the bar, then he walked over and picked up the six-shooter. "You can get it back at the sheriff's office when you're ready to leave town."

"Yeah." He poured a drink and gulped it down. "You know something, Sheriff?"

"I told you I'm the deputy."

"You know something, Deputy?" the man said, wincing in pain.

"What?"

"You oughta use your pistol more. You're gonna kill somebody with that club o' yours one o' these days," he advised.

"I bent the barrel of a good Colt on some son of a bitch with a hard head," Guy said. "From now on I use my billy made outta jirara wood."

Guy left the saloon and resumed his walk to the local lockup. When he reached it, he went inside, and stopped short at the sight of the man sitting at the desk in front of the place's two empty cells.

Captain Charlie Delano leisurely smoked a cigar, his feet up on the desk. "Howdy, Guy."

"Howdy, Cap'n Delano," Guy said. He walked over to a gun cabinet and unlocked the drawer beneath the rifle rack. He put the confiscated pistol in and locked it up. "What brings you to Sweetwater?"

"Why, Guy Tyrone, I wanted to see you," Delano said.

"You got a warrant on me?"

"Should I?" Delano asked.

"Well—" Guy grabbed a chair and positioned it next to the desk. "I'm wanted in the Injun Territory."

"You know I'm a Texas Ranger," Delano said. "I got no jurisdiction in the Injun country."

"There's some folks in Arkansas that might like to have a word or two with me," Tyrone pointed out cautiously.

"Same thing," Delano said.

"And about a half-dozen counties in Texas," Guy added.

"Now, Guy, that's differ'nt," Delano said.

Guy decided not to speak anymore. He figured it would be better to see what Delano had to say.

"You been on all sides o' the law, haven't you?" Delano remarked. "Bottom and top too, if there is one.

"It just depends," Guy said.

"I was looking all over for you, then I heard you was a deputy sheriff in Sweetwater," Delano said. "So I decided to come and give you a friendly howdy."

"Howdy," Guy said dully.

"Howdy," Delano said.

Guy came to the point. "Are you gonna arrest me, Cap'n? I gotta know because—"

"Nope," Delano interrupted. "I'm gonna do two things. First off, I'm letting you know that I'm sending a telegraph this very day, and have ever' damn warrant out for your ass taken off the books and put away forever."

"Can you do that?" Guy asked, brightening up.

"Sure can," Delano said. "I got special authorization to do a coupla things I might want to do."

"That'd be right nice o' you, Cap'n," Guy remarked. Then he asked suspiciously, "What's the second thing you're gonna do?"

"Enlist you in the Texas Rangers," Delano replied.

"Why?" Guy wanted to know.

"To go on a special case with me," Guy said. "If things work out and you decide to stay, you can go into the Frontier Battalion and be a regular Ranger."

"I don't want to talk 'bout no Frontier Battalions," Guy said. "I want to talk about that special case."

"Sure," Delano said. "By the way—do you still carry that club 'o yours?"

"The one made outta jirara wood—the hardest wood knowed to man?" Guy said. "Sure. As a matter o' fact, I just dusted off a feller's head with it." He reached down and grabbed it, proudly showing off the wooden weapon.

"Can you still throw it and hit a fly on the wall?" Delano asked.

"I'm as sharp as ever," Guy assured him.

"Well, you can put it away," Charlie said. "There's gonna be a hell of a lot more call for shooting than hitting."

"It's only good to use in town," Guy admitted. "Anyhow, let's get back to that case.

Delano shifted his feet to make himself more comfortable. "Have you ever heard of Ace Erickson?"

"I heard tell of a feller over to Stavanger that goes by that name," Guy said.

Delano looked Guy straight in the eye with a glare

that almost made the deputy wince. "You ever work for him?"

Guy cleared his throat. "I'd be the last to deny I ain't had my problems with the law in certain parts, Cap'n. Ain't I always told you the truth about that?"

"Sure," Delano said. "Answer my question. Have you ever worked for Ace Erickson?"

"Come on, Cap'n!" Guy protested. "All I ever done in my life is get drunk and jump into fights. Disturbing the peace is the worst I done."

"You done that good a coupla times as I recollect," Delano pointed out.

"Yeah. But I never been a thief or a killer," Guy said. "The onliest men I've shot was shooting at me."

"I just wanted to make sure you wouldn't have no divided loyalties," Delano said.

"Now you know," Guy said.

Further conversation was cut off when the door of the office opened and the man Guy had clubbed in the saloon walked in.

"I been thinking about you," he said, glaring at Guy.

"It's nice to be remembered," Guy said. "You want your iron back?"

"Yeah," the man said. "And I want it now."

Guy shook his head. "I don't think so."

"You said I could have it back when I left town," the man said.

"Maybe I did," Guy said. "But I'm feeling kinda nervous 'bout handing it over. What's your name?"

"None o' your damn business!"

"Get the hell outta here," Guy said. "I'll think on giving you back your pistol tomorrow—maybe."

The man drew fast, dragging the Remington .44 from beneath his vest. "Both o' you son of a bitches raise 'em!"

Delano and Guy put their hands up.

"Undo them gun belts and kick 'em in that far cell," the man said. He grinned. "By the way, since you asked, my name is Ed Hall."

"Howdy, Ed," Tyrone said.

"You ain't gonna be such a funny boy in a coupla minutes," Hall promised him. He waited while they obeyed him. "Now pull off that club o' yours and drop it on the floor and roll it my way."

Guy did as he was told. "Anything else, Ed?"

"I got something for your pal to do," Hall said. He picked up the club and motioned to Delano with it. "Get in that other cell." He waited until Delano obeyed. "Lock them doors," Hall told Guy. "And throw the keys over in the corner."

"Sure, Ed."

Hall shoved the pistol back in his belt and advanced toward Guy. "Now I'm gonna slam-bang the cowpiss outta you!"

He took a couple of wild swings with the club, but Guy ducked under the attack. He whipped his fist around and caught Hall in the ribs with a vicious punch.

"Oof!" Hall swung again, this time connecting with Guy's left shoulder.

"Ow!"

"Hardest wood knowed to man, huh?" Hall crowed. He charged again, swinging in vicious, swift arcs.

Guy danced away, barely keeping out of harm's way. He finally feinted a couple of times in every direction he could manage, then lunged upward, grasping Hall's wrist.

"Goddamn you!" Hall swore. He reached up to grab the club with his other hand.

Guy banged him on the skull with his own head,

the collision making a loud cracking sound. Both fighters were stunned as the club fell clattering to the floor. Dazed and lurching, both men tried to get the wooden weapon. They accidentally kicked it into the cell with Delano.

Hall punched Guy hard, driving him over the top of the desk and to the floor on the other side. The larger, heavier man went to the attack and dived over the scarred hunk of furniture, crashing onto Guy's skinny body.

Guy tried to get up, but a couple more hard punches kept him from being able to put up a lot of fight. But by kicking out suddenly and viciously, he got free. Hall was fast, closing in and grabbing the deputy in a bear hug. Once more they went to the floor, and Guy began getting the worst of it.

The shot blasted out, the loudness intensified in the confines of the jail office.

"Hold it!" Delano bellowed. "That's enough!"

Both combatants looked over to see the Ranger captain holding a small Smith & Wesson .38 revolver, a wisp of smoke coming from its barrel.

"Fight's over," Delano said. He glared at Hall. "If you blink an eye in a way that don't please me, I'll shoot it out."

Hall put his hands up as Guy reached under the man's belt and pulled his Remington free. The deputy looked at Delano. "Did you have that backup gun all the time?"

"Sure," Delano said cheerfully. "Now get the keys and open up the cells. I'll get out while Mr. Hall here gets in."

Within moments the new prisoner was freshly lodged and the office back to normal. Delano reached in his jacket pocket and pulled out a badge. "This here is the official sign o' the Texas Rangers," he announced. "Now raise your hand while I swear you in."

Breathing hard with a bleeding nose and blackened eye, Guy did as he was told. "How come I feel that this ain't the smartest thing I'm ever gonna do?"

"Shut up and repeat after me," Delano said. "I swear . . ."

Two

The cabin was barely visible down in the draw. The light just before dawn was dim. The view was further obscured by a mist from the nearby river that drifted slowly in the light breezes that hardly stirred as much as a blade of grass.

Up on the higher ground, his Winchester ready at his side, Deputy United States Marshal Gideon Magee lightly rubbed his hands together to step up the circulation and hold off the early morning chill. Gideon was a big, heavy man with coal-black hair and bushy eyebrows that gave his face a perpetual look of ferocity. A heavy mustache drooped from beneath a bulbous nose and his collar was buttoned around a thick, bull neck.

Gideon was as tired, hungry, and mad as a wolf in winter. He'd trailed the three men from Pawhuska to Muskogee, then up to Vinita in the Cherokee Nation, and finally back east a ways more to where he now looked down on them.

The deputy marshal worked out of Judge Isaac Parker's federal court in Fort Smith, Arkansas. That was situated in the northern part of the state with only the Arkansas River between it and Indian Territory. The judge was charged with administering justice for crimes committed in the Indian country. Gideon Magee and his ilk earned their pay by going out into that vast, dangerous wilderness and bringing the criminals back to justice.

And that's what he was doing on that ridge staring down at the dilapidated cabin.

The three murdering horse thieves inside hadn't led Gideon on a hell of a chase by accident or blind, unthinking luck. Once they'd figured out it was him on their trail, they rode like the devil himself was trying to grab their horses' tails. Marshal Gideon Magee, in twenty years of serving as an officer of various branches of the law, had brought back only a half-dozen live prisoners. He was known among those on the owlhoot trail to shoot first, then order hands to be raised. That was the sort of man they respected and feared.

Gideon shifted his weight and continued to watch the hovel. The trio's mounts were stabled in a lean-to not far from the front door. He had thought of running the animals off, but going down there would have put him in a bad spot. He enjoyed plenty of cover where he was, so he bided his time waiting to see what would happen.

Gideon would have liked to enjoy a smoke on his pipe, but he knew there was a good chance one of his quarry might be looking out for trouble and spot the glare of the match when he lit up.

The sun climbed a bit higher, edging through the top of the trees to throw more light on the scene. The outlaws were sleeping late. That made Gideon grin. Their tiredness was a sure sign he'd been running the sons of bitches 'til they were worn down, tuckered out, and used up.

A movement below caught his eye. The cabin door had shaken a bit. Someone was taking a cautious look out. A minute later a figure appeared, then edged along the front of the place and stopped at the corner. Another quick look around was followed by a hurried piss. After relieving himself, the man scooted back inside.

Gideon could have shot him, but he wanted all three outside in the open before any gunplay broke out.

A few muffled sounds now came from the interior. That meant they were up and stirring around. The door opened again. Once more there was a cautious exit to tend to nature's call. As soon as the second man went inside, the third scooted out. Another wetting of the Indian Territory and once more all three were out of sight within the cabin.

Another quarter of an hour eased by before any more action became evident. Two of the outlaws came outside carrying their saddles. They walked a few paces, then stopped when the third appeared in the doorway. A conversation ensued, and Gideon finally deducted that the two were going to make a run for it and the third had decided to stick out in the cabin for a while.

Gideon raised the carbine to his shoulder and took aim.

The first shot hit its target. The outlaw lurched forward and fell to his knees. Gideon was too hasty on the second. The bullet hit the next man's saddle, knocking it from his arms. He left it and sprinted for his horse. By then the shot man had died on his knees and pitched over on his face.

A slug whacked the rocks near Gideon. The man inside the cabin had spotted him. Gideon pulled back in time to see the other fellow who had gone outside streak into view on his horse, riding desperately and bareback as he made a run for freedom.

It took Gideon three bullets to knock him from his mount. The horse thief's body bounced and rolled into a rocky little creek. Now the deputy marshal turned his attention back to the cabin.

All was quiet.

Once more Gideon settled down for a wait. There was no place for the man to go. If he tried his horse, he would die like the others. A rush outside would mean joining the fellow lying facedown in front of the cabin. It looked like Judge Parker would have one less case to try. At least he'd be saved from sentencing a hanging from that particular fiasco.

The bullet whipped by Gideon's face so fast he swore it took some hairs of his mustache with it. He rolled over and brought the carbine to bear at the exact moment the outlaw fired again. Gideon shot back, scrambling to his left until he found a fallen log to give him cover.

"Damn me for a fool!" Gideon hissed aloud.

He realized the surviving outlaw had made a break from the cabin and headed up the draw straight at him while he was gunning down the shithead trying to ride off bareback.

Another shot blasted in the closeness of the trees. "Hey, you, Magee!" the horse thief yelled out with a crackle.

Gideon recognized the voice. Ben Cornel was an old adversary.

"Answer me, Magee!" Cornel yelled again.

Gideon kept quiet. Cornel was a small, physically powerful man who would be able to move swiftly and effortlessly through the trees that grew thick above the draw. The deputy marshal, on the other hand, was not noted for his grace. Large and heavy, he could be downright clumsy at times.

"Them two was scared o' you, Magee!" Cornel

yelled. "But I ain't, you old bastard! I'm gonna shoot you like a hog for supper!"

Gideon didn't like his position. The log offered cover only on one side. If Cornel moved swiftly, and there was no doubt he would, he could be behind him in a matter of moments with a clear shot at the hapless marshal.

"C'mon, Magee. Talk to me!"

The lawman got to his hands and knees. He slowly crawled backward, keeping his ears cocked for any noise. When he reached a stand of trees with heavy brush around their base, he moved inside the cover and watched.

A large hunk of bark flew off near his head as a bullet slammed into the tree.

"I see you, Magee!" Cornel yelled. "You can't get away!"

Gideon, desperate, made a run in the opposite direction. He crashed through the brush with thorns tearing at his clothes. Suddenly he stepped out into thin air, then fell. Running blindly through the thick vegetation, he'd gone off the edge of the draw and now tumbled and rolled to the bottom. Each blow of his powerful body against the steeply sloped ground took some breath away until he reached the bottom. But his Winchester was still clutched tightly in his hand.

Gideon lay stunned for a few moments, trying to get himself collected and back in order. He was on his back, his feet pointing away from the dirt wall of the canyonlike feature. He glanced upward and saw Cornel peering down, trying to spot him. Gideon raised the carbine and, aiming upside down, made a desperate shot.

The bullet went in the bottom part of Ben Cornel's jaw and blew his hat—and the top of his head—

straight up into the air. The outlaw made a graceful forward fall, coming off the rim of the draw and bouncing all the way to the bottom just as Gideon had done.

Now the marshal laboriously got to his feet. He walked over to Cornel and winced at the sight of the dead man's sunken face. The top of his skull was a red mush.

"Did you want to talk to me, Cornel?" Gideon asked of the dead man. "I think you wanted me to answer you or something." He kicked the corpse. "You'll have to excuse me. I got things to tend to."

It took a half hour to gather up the horses, including the one that had been used for the bareback escape attempt, and bring them together.

Gideon threw a body over each animal, securing it with rope he kept in his saddlebags for just such a purpose. When all was ready, he retrieved his own roan and came back to gather up the others for the ride back to Fort Smith.

The trip through the dipping terrain of eastern Indian Territory was uneventful except that Cornel's body slipped around to hang under his horse on one occasion. Gideon had to stop and readjust the corpse.

"Goddamn you, Cornel," he said as he struggled with the weight of the dead man. "Always giving me fits. And you ain't stopped even after you're dead. Hell, you're drawing flies, you son of a bitch."

After making sure the cadaver would stay in place, Gideon remounted and continued the slow trek back to civilization. Late that same afternoon he and the animals clopped across the bridge spanning the Arkansas River and brought the morbid cargo into the town of Fort Smith.

A couple of loafers on the street hollered over at him as he passed by. "Hey, Marshal Magee! Got some more that didn't know how to quit, huh?"

"I reckon you don't even bother to carry handcuffs, do you, Marshal Magee?"

Gideon ignored the gibes as he went straight down the street to the local undertaking parlor. As usual he went around the back, emitting a loud whistle when he arrived.

The door opened and the mortician, a tall, thin man named Hanks, stepped out. He looked over the load. "Three this time, Marshal?"

"It looks that way," Gideon answered. "They ain't gonna be worth much to you. It don't look like they owned much o' anything. You'll have to settle for the burying bill."

"It'll do," Hanks replied. He yelled out for help, and a couple of his assistants emerged from the undertaking parlor. Without a word between them, they went to work dragging the three dead men from the animals and taking them inside.

"What about them horses?" Hanks asked.

"They're stole," Gideon said. "And branded. I reckon they'll be claimed by their owners."

Hanks shrugged. "Then I reckon you're right. The onliest pay I'll get will be for burying 'em. Anyhow, I'm 'bliged."

"You're welcome," Gideon said.

The marshal rode back to the street and turned toward the livery stable where the government horses were kept. After turning in the roan, he got his saddlebags and headed toward the boardinghouse where he had a room. The exhaustion was really setting in then, and all Gideon wanted was to get some hot food in his belly, take a bath, then sleep for a week.

But his landlady, Mrs. Nivens, had news when he arrived. "They say there's a telegram for you at the courthouse."

"I'll get it tomorrow," Gideon said. "Can you fix something to eat?"

"They said the telegram is important," Mrs. Nivens said.

"A stack o' pancakes and ham would be pure nice," Gideon said.

"They said it come all the way from Texas," Mrs. Nivens said.

"Your boy around?" Gideon asked.

Mrs. Nivens turned and yelled out, "Orville!"

A moment later a quick and obedient twelve-year-old appeared in the yard where they stood.

"Orville," Gideon said wearily. "Go on down to the courthouse and fetch that telegram they got for me."

"Yes, sir, Marshal Magee!" The boy was off and down the street in an instant.

"Now, Mrs. Nivens, can I have them pancakes?" Gideon asked.

"Certainly, Marshal Magee."

He went up to his room and dropped off his saddlebags in the corner, then went back downstairs to the kitchen. By the time he settled down, Orville was back with the telegram. Gideon wordlessly took it and unfolded the missive.

Mrs. Nivens looked back from the counter where she had begun to mix the batter for the pancakes. "Is it from a friend o' yours?"

"Yeah," Gideon answered. "A cap'n in the Texas Rangers."

"Now that's nice," she said. "I hope it's good news."

Gideon refolded the telegram and stuck it in his shirt pocket. "After I eat, I'll like a bath."

"I'll have Orville heat up some water, Marshal Magee," Mrs. Nivens said.

"Then I reckon I'll go and sleep 'til the morning,"

Gideon said. "I'll be leaving sometime tomorrow. You can shut up my room for a while."

"Are you going off again, Marshal?" the landlady asked.

"Yes, ma'am," Gideon said wearily. "To Texas."

Three

Ace Erickson ran the brush through his hair, then stepped back to study the effect in the mirror. "You think I'm going bald?" He was a tall slim man in his late thirties with Scandinavian good looks.

Dinah Walters, a beautiful woman with black hair and striking green eyes, looked over from the sofa where she sat. "You got lots o' hair, Ace."

He studied himself some more. "Mmm! I don't know. It appears thinner to me."

"You're a handsome man," Dinah said sincerely. Back east, with a better opportunity to be stylish or even go on the stage, she would have been a striking beauty pursued and admired by wealthy men. But on the frontier Dinah was far short of her potential. But, even in those circumstances, the woman had done very well for herself.

Ace laid the brush down on the dressing table and walked across his living room to where his coat hung. The apartment was above his saloon in Stavanger, Texas. The place was called the Ace of Diamonds and was the only drinking establishment in the town. "Are your gals ready for tonight?"

"They're always ready, Ace, honey," she replied. Dinah bossed the dancehall girls who furnished entertainment to the customers. Her position of authority meant she didn't take any of the clients upstairs to the dozen rooms set aside for such business. Ace paid her well because she was an excellent hostess and kept things in good running order. It was said that Dinah Walters could charm a preacher into downing a bottle of rye whiskey.

"The boys are coming in, Dinah," he said. "Didn't I tell you?"

"No, you didn't." When Ace talked about *the* boys, he meant his main group of marauders who usually spent their time out on T. J. Grogan's ranch between jobs. When it came to entertainment, they were a demanding bunch. "How many of them?" she asked.

"The whole damn bunch," he answered. "They performed quite well on the last job. It's time to give them an evening or two here in Stavanger with some good liquor and decent-looking women, or I'm going to have a mutiny on my hands."

"I might have to bring in some extra girls," Dinah said. "At least I will if your men stick around for any time."

"They won't be here for more than a couple of days," Ace remarked. "It's dangerous to keep them so close around here. It attracts too much attention." He winked at her. "Anyhow, you'll figure things out." He slipped into his coat and went back to the mirror. He adjusted the handkerchief in the pocket, then picked up an ace of diamond card from the small table in front of him. He stuck it in the pocket as well, adjusting it in front of the handkerchief.

"You never forget that card, do you?" Dinah remarked.

It was an old custom of Ace Erickson's that had earned him his moniker. "I always like to have that ace with me," he said. "No matter what happens, it gives me the feeling like I still got a fighting chance." He glanced out the window. "The sun's going down."

"That means the day's work is about to begin," Dinah said.

"Then let's go," Ace said. "Tune the piano, pour the liquor, and start the fun." He went to the door and opened it, holding it for her. "After you."

"You're such a gentleman," Dinah said lightly, laying her hand on his face as she walked past him.

They went down the stairs to the nearly empty saloon. The place would be crowded within a couple of hours, but at that moment things were quiet. The bartender loafed at his post while a couple of drinkers treated themselves to occasional swallows of whiskey. One of them looked up at the couple's appearance. He smiled at Dinah.

"Hello, Gustavo," she said.

Sheriff Gustavo Fairweather, the town's only lawman, nodded past her at Ace Erickson. He was responsible for closing down all the competing saloons while Ace organized his hold on the town of Stavanger. After that, Fairweather made sure that any other law officers investigating the goings-on in the town were kept as much in the dark as possible or ended up with a bullet in their back if they pried too deeply. After less than a year, Stavanger belonged to Ace Erickson lock, stock, and saloon.

"How's things look, Sheriff?" Ace asked.

"I got it all under control," Fairweather replied. "Are the boys still coming in?"

"Yeah," Ace replied. "They did a good job. And

I've been real happy with Ned Paulson. He's kept things under control out there as well as you've done here."

"That's why I recommended him, Ace," Fairweather said.

"Well, boys, I have things to do," Dinah said. "I'll be seeing you later." She went on to check her dance-hall-girl crew while Ace Erickson walked across the saloon to his office. He stepped inside and nodded to the man sitting there. "How are you doing, Max? You're in a little early, aren't you?"

Maxwell Banter, Ace's attorney, looked up from the paper he was reading. "Good evening, Ace. I'm restless," Banter replied. "The sooner we see the results of the last job, the sooner I can relax. And I heard that the boys are coming in tonight."

"That's right," Ace Erickson said, sitting behind the desk.

"It would seem they scored big on that Wells Fargo shipment," Banter said.

"Good planning," Ace said with a wink.

"Good information," Banter said back to him.

"A little of both," Ace said.

"A *lot* of both," Banter replied.

Ace Erickson grinned. "We're a good team, aren't we?" He opened the large desk drawer and pulled out an accounting book. He opened it and began to enter figures from some scraps of paper he retrieved from his pocket. "How's that warrant in Austin doing? I don't want to have any problems with a marshal or ranger coming out here looking for Ned Paulson."

"I got a letter today," Maxwell Banter said. "It's been withdrawn. Something about lack of evidence."

"Something about a payoff," Ace said.

"It's not cheap doing business with the state judiciary," Banter reminded him.

"Just the same, after the boys have been here a couple of days, I'm going to send them out to Grogan's. It'll take several weeks to let things cool down," Ace said. "They can stay out at the ranch to wait for the next job."

"Good idea," Banter said. "And that gives me faith in you, Ace. You've got an intelligently applied patience when it comes to working these jobs."

"That's why I've never seen the inside of a jail," Ace said. He finished entering the figures, then began adding them up. He worked rapidly, his quick mind calculating the numbers without error all the way to the bottom of the column.

"How's it look?" Maxwell Banter asked.

"Everything tallies," Ace said. "You can always tell the books are right when I don't decide to shoot somebody."

"Remember that I'm your attorney not your accountant," Banter said a bit nervously. "Particularly when those figures don't come out right."

"Sure, Max," Ace said.

The sound of horses' hooves floated faintly from the saloon into the office. Within moments it was louder, then gruff voices could be heard as the clatter and bumping of several horsemen coming to a halt was easily discernible.

"They're here," Banter said.

Ace Erickson got up from behind the desk and walked to the office door. He pushed it open and stood there waiting until a half-dozen dusty, trail-weary men strode into the saloon. Their boots clomped on the wooden flooring and their spurs jangled. The acrid smell of campfire smoke filled the place.

"Paulson!" Ace shouted.

One of the arriving men stepped out from the throng. He spotted Ace in the doorway. Waving a greeting, he strode rapidly over to him. "Howdy, Boss."

"Come on in and let's have a drink," Ace Erickson said.

Ned Paulson had a pair of saddlebags thrown over his shoulder. He went inside the office and dropped them on the desk. "Howdy, Mr. Banter."

"Hello, Ned," Maxwell Banter said.

Ace went to the bags and opened them up. He pulled out several large leather pouches. Then he loosened the drawstring on one and dumped it out. Twenty-dollar gold pieces bounced and rolled on the desk.

"Good haul, Boss," Paulson said.

"I'll say," Ace agreed. He motioned to a liquor cabinet by the wall. "Pour us three big straight ones, Ned."

"You bet, Boss." The man complied, serving the other two first before filling a tumbler with whiskey for himself.

"How'd the job go?" Ace Erickson asked.

"Well—" Paulson hesitated. "We had to shoot one o' the baggage guards."

"Goddamn it!" Ace swore.

"We couldn't help it, Boss! The son of a bitch had throwed down on Shorty," Paulson explained. "If Tolliver hadn't shot him, we'd've lost Shorty."

Banter slowly shook his head. "Murder is hard to fix, Ace," he said. "In fact, it's damn near impossible."

"Well, hell!" Paulson protested. "We didn't want to lose Shorty, did we?"

Ace held up his hand. "You did the right thing, Ned. Don't worry."

Paulson grinned with relief and took a drink. "How'd that warrant turn out?"

"It's gone away," Banter answered. "At least we're done with the problem. You won't have anyone coming into Denton County looking for you."

"Maybe," Paulson said. "And maybe not. Who's gonna serve a warrant here in Stavanger? Especially with Gustavo Fairweather on the job here."

"The trouble is that you boys aren't always here in Stavanger," Ace Erickson said. "That's why I want you to be careful out on the ranch too."

Maxwell Banter shook his head. "I'm worried about this new problem. Shooting a Wells Fargo guard is bad business."

"I was thinking of letting things simmer down for a couple of weeks anyhow," Ace said. "A bit of delay will fit into our schedule anyway."

"You want us to go to Grogan's?" Paulson asked.

"Yeah," Ace replied. "And from now on I want you and the boys to plan on going there after every job. It will be safer to use it as a hideout, especially after that guard was killed."

"You bet, Boss," Paulson said. "By the way, do you have any more jobs lined up for us?"

"Yeah, as a matter of fact we've got word on a bank shipment by stage out of Lubbock in a few weeks," Ace Erickson said. "Greenbacks," he added.

"I prefer gold pieces," Paulson said, pointing at the desk. "But I reckon paper money is good sometimes too."

"It is in the better circles of society," Banter pointed out.

"I ain't hardly going to them parts, Mr. Banter," Paulson said with a grin. "But I reckon just about any sporting gal this side o' the Staked Plains is gonna come across for it."

Maxwell Banter sipped the whiskey. "I envy you at times, Ned. Sometimes I wish those more basic things would satisfy what aches in my soul."

Paulson, in spite of a lack of education and a simplistic view of life, understood. "If you'd been borned in a soddy like me and raised on turnips and what game could be shot, you'd be happy with just about anything too."

Ace laughed. "You're a long way from Long Island, aren't you, Max?"

Banter smiled wistfully. "I'll go back someday. Or at least to a life similar to what unhappy circumstances drove me from."

"There's a statute of limitations on embezzlement, isn't there?" Ace asked.

"Certainly," Banter said. "But that doesn't mean one can go back to the community where the embezzlement occurred."

"What's em-bezzel-whatta-ya-call-it?" Paulson asked.

"As a young attorney I represented a wealthy client's business interests over a period of years," Maxwell Banter said. "Let's just say I tapped the till to rush myself to a lifestyle to which I would have reached rather slowly had I been more honest."

Paulson, who knew what a holdup was or a cattle-rustling foray, didn't care to delve into Banter's past.

The man never did come out and say things straight anyhow. He looked at Ace. "Do you want anything else, Boss?"

"No," Ace Erickson said. "We'll divvy the loot tomorrow after it's all accounted for."

"It's there, Boss," Paulson assured him. "Ever' last gold piece."

"We'll know if it's short," Banter assured him. "We set up the deal, remember?"

"Yeah. I remember, Mr. Banter." He drained the tumbler of whiskey and set it back on the liquor cabinet. "Well, Dinah's gals are out there just waiting. I reckon I'll have me some fun 'til we got to leave Stavanger."

"Enjoy yourself, Ned," Ace said.

The outlaw left the two men to go join the celebration in the saloon.

Ace settled himself behind the desk again. "How long do you think this setup of ours is going to go on?"

Maxwell Banter laughed. "You're a pessimist, aren't you?"

"I'm a realist, Max," Ace said.

"Well, relax," Banter assured him. "We've got so many politicians and judges paid off that if a serious investigation got under way, the scrambling around to get out of the way would kick up enough dust for us to hide behind for years."

"I've been out west longer than you," Ace Erickson said. "I've seen how things are handled when certain types decide the situation has gone on long enough."

"But that was a few years ago," Banter argued. "Civilization is advancing on us, Ace. And the more civilizing goes on, the easier it is to use systems that grow more complicated and cumbersome. You leave all that to me."

"That's fine and you're good at it," Ace said. "But one of these days, some hairy-eared, tobacco-chewing son of a bitch is going to come into Stavanger with nothing but guts, guns, and a tin star."

"I'll let you handle that if it happens," Banter said.

"Don't worry," Ace assured him. "I've always got an ace up my sleeve."

"You mean in your pocket," Maxwell Banter said with a chuckle.

"Come on," Ace Erickson said. "Let's join the boys and watch them loosen up."

"Yeah," Banter said. "That's always amusing."

The two left the office and joined the boisterous crowd at the bar.

Four

Captain Charlie Delano and Ranger Guy Tyrone slowly walked up and down the Dallas depot platform. They didn't speak to each other. Instead, side by side, the two men went about their pacing without as much as a word between them. Each was lost in his own thoughts about the difficult and dangerous job that lay ahead.

Across the tracks the outer edges of the community spread out, growing sparser until only occasional shacks appeared out on the prairie.

"Gideon must have had a hell of trip," Guy remarked, breaking their self-imposed silence. "He ain't gonna be in a good humor when he gets here."

"I never knowed him to be a pleasant feller under any circumstances," Charlie remarked.

"Getting here from Fort Smith means riverboat, stage, and finally train," Guy said. "That's a hell of a lot o' travel trouble." He rubbed his chin. "Nope. He ain't gonna be in a good mood a'tall."

"He answered my telegram quick enough," Charlie pointed out. "I knew he'd been working out o' Judge Parker's court for a spell. So he's ready for a change. He's the kind that can't stay put for long."

A whistle in the distance marked the approach of the train. Now a few more people appeared from the waiting room as they came out either to get aboard as passengers or to meet travelers arriving at Dallas.

Guy stuck his hand in his vest pocket and idly toyed with the Texas Ranger badge he'd stuck there. Charlie Delano didn't want them displaying any authority unless it was absolutely necessary. But there was something about that star that gave him an extra sense of pride he'd never felt as a town deputy.

It took a quarter hour for the engine to finally come over the horizon under a plume of streaming black smoke. It sped on in toward Dallas, the whistle blasting now and then. When it was close enough, the engineer cut the steam and started hauling on the brakes. The result was a hissing, clanging, loudly squeaking arrival that sounded like the yelling of enraged banshees. The locomotive stopped as if under protest, sparks flying from wheels thrown into reverse, as it resisted the momentous push of the cars it hauled.

Then all was quiet except for hissing of escaping steam from safety valves.

More activity broke out in the vicinity as a depot clerk wheeled a baggage cart out to collect cargo. The train wasn't scheduled to tarry long before heading out for points to the southwest. Passengers with tickets hurried to get aboard while the people just arriving began to step down wearily from the cars, displaying that stiffness that all travelers have after being confined aboard cars for a length of time.

"There he is," Charlie said.

Guy looked and could see the large figure of Gideon Magee clump down from a passenger car's step. Gideon looked around, then spotted them. He walked toward them in his lumbering style, carrying a carpetbag valise with him.

Charlie offered his hand. "Glad to see you, Gideon."

"Same here, Charlie," Gideon said. He looked at Guy Tyrone. "Are you with Charlie or does he have you under arrest?"

Guy grinned. "I'm with him." He also shook hands with the big man. "I'm a Texas Ranger," he added in a whisper.

Gideon looked at him, then at Charlie. "Is that right?"

"Yeah," Charlie answered.

"Damn!" Gideon said. He abruptly changed the subject. "Where we going from here?" Gideon asked.

"The Windsor Hotel," Charlie answered. "We can chew the fat once we're there."

"I don't want to do no visiting 'til I'm settled in a room and had a hot bath. I been moving day and night since I left Fort Smith. So after I'm soaked and unstiffened, it's down to the bar to cut five days' travel outta my throat with good whiskey," Gideon said.

"C'mon then," Charlie Delano said. "We'll head for the Windsor."

"The Windsor, huh?" Gideon Magee remarked. "Then the State o' Texas must be paying the bill."

"You got it right," Charlie said. "But I gotta warn you. We ain't gonna be staying there long."

They went down a short set of stairs that led from the platform to the ground. Charlie and Guy took Gideon over to a hitching rail where three horses stood waiting.

"The middle one's yours," Guy said.

Gideon unlooped the reins, stepped into the left stirrup, and pulled himself into the saddle while holding onto the valise in one hand. "Let's go," he said. "My ass ain't taking to this saddle any better'n it did a train seat." Since he knew his way around Dallas, he didn't wait for the others. Gideon rode off for the business section and the Windsor Hotel.

"Hey!" Charlie yelled out. "We ain't taking the horses to the room. There's a livery stable on the street behind the hotel."

"I know which one it is," Gideon Magee called back. He kicked the horse into a canter and went on with his friends following.

By the time Charlie Delano and Guy Tyrone arrived, Gideon already had the horse in a stable and was pulling the saddle off to set it on the stall wall. "What's taking you two so long?" he asked.

"I'll take care o' the horses," Guy said. "Take him up to the room and get him that damn bath or he ain't gonna be fit company to be with."

Charlie and Gideon walked out of the large barn and crossed the street. They strolled rapidly around to the other side of the block with Gideon a couple of steps ahead. They went straight into the lobby, and Charlie came to an abrupt halt.

Gideon Magee stopped and turned around. "What the hell're you waiting for?"

"I just want to see what room you're fixing to charge into," Charlie said. "Are you gonna just take one that suits you, or go to ours?"

"I ain't in no mood for joking. I told you I

wanted a hot bath then down to the bar," Gideon said. "And I want it in a hurry. So just tell me where we're bunking."

"We're on the third floor," Captain Charlie Delano said now leading the way. He passed the desk and signaled to the clerk. "We'll take hot water for a bath in 304."

"Right away, Captain!"

Gideon, now in a slightly better mood, followed. When they reached the room, he went to the bed indicated as his and set his valise down. He treated himself to a bone-cracking stretch and a loud yawn as Charlie settled down in a chair by the window.

Guy came through the door and noted Gideon standing there. "Make yourself comfortable, Gideon."

"I'm fixing to make myself comfortable in a tub o' hot water," Gideon Magee said testily.

Guy went over to his bed and sat down on it. "They got good service in this hotel."

As if to prove him right, there was a knock on the door. Charlie opened and admitted five bellboys. Two wrestled with a copper tub, another carried two pails of hot water, the fourth had one pail of hot water and one pail of cold water, and the fifth had soap and a towel. Rapidly and efficiently, they set the bath up in the corner of the room in a matter of minutes. Charlie tipped them while Gideon stripped off his clothes and tested the water.

"Perfect!" Gideon said, settling in.

Charlie went to his bedstand and poured a glassful of Kentucky bourbon. He took it over to Gideon. "You might as well start cutting them five days' travel right now."

"I'll agree with that," Gideon Magee said. He

took the tumbler and drained it in three swallows. "Would one o' you fetch my pipe outta that valise?"

Charlie Delano retrieved the pipe while Guy Tyrone came over with a match. Within moments, Gideon was washing vigorously and smoking as he soaped down. When he was clean, he settled back to soak a bit. "Can I have another o' your bourbons, Charlie?"

"Sure," Charlie said. He fixed the drink. "Don't take all night. We got to go to work tomorrow."

"Will we be able to talk in the hotel bar?" Gideon asked. He finished off the bourbon. "Your telegram made some strong hints about being quiet about this thing we're going into."

"We can sit in a corner and not be bothered by nobody," Guy told him.

Gideon looked at his companions and sensed their impatience. "Aw, hell!" He stood up and grabbed the towel, rubbing himself dry. After dressing quickly, he brushed his hair. "That's it, boys. I'm anxious to hear what you've got to say."

The trio of lawmen went down to the lobby and crossed it to the establishment's saloon. They went to the back of the room and placed their orders with a waiter. None bothered to talk much until they'd been served and left alone.

Gideon Magee looked at Charlie. "So? How's come you dragged me all the way down here, Charlie?"

Charlie was efficient with his words as he told of Ace Erickson and his criminal headquarters in Stavanger. The Ranger captain didn't leave out the crooked lawyer Maxwell Banter or Sheriff Gustavo Fairweather.

"Fairweather!" Gideon exclaimed. "I thought that son of a bitch was in the territorial prison in Montana."

"He escaped," Charlie Delano said.

"Then let's send him back," Gideon said. Then he added, "Or shoot him."

"That is one of the things we're planning on doing," Charlie said. Then he delved into the nastier parts of the job. He told Gideon Magee that if any of them were caught and taken to trial, the governor and his office would not help them a bit. He concluded with, "And I'm gonna swear you into the Rangers. At least you'll get paid that way."

"I'm still a deputy U.S. marshal," Gideon Magee pointed out. "I only took a leave of absence from Judge Parker's court."

Guy laughed. "When the time comes to pack a star, you can pin two of 'em on your vest."

"I'll just do that," Gideon said. He turned back to Charlie. "So what're we gonna do, Charlie? Move into Stavanger and call out this Ace Erickson?"

Charlie shook his head. "Nope. This is one time when we kill the snake by going for his body 'stead of his head."

Guy frowned in puzzlement. "Why? Wouldn't it wrap things up right quick if we got Erickson?"

"Wouldn't solve nothing much," Charlie Delano said. "That'd leave the lawyer Banter and Fairweather alive and kicking. And if we got them two, then that'd leave a whole bandit gang running loose."

"I see what you're driving at, Charlie," Gideon said. "If we knock off the gang, then Erickson and his top dogs won't have their army no more."

"That's right," Charlie said. "Then we move in on them for the final showdown."

"The gang don't stay in Stavanger, does it?" Guy Tyrone remarked. "That means we'll be spending a lot o' time in the open country."

"That's where they hide out," Charlie said. "And that's where we'll have to go to find 'em."

"Well, hell, Charlie!" Gideon said in exasperation. "We can't just ride out into the wide open spaces and start looking for 'em. We might never find them owlhoots."

"I got us a place to start," Charlie said. "The gang holes up at a ranch between jobs. They only go into Stavanger to split the take or for a little relaxation now and then."

"Where's this ranch?" Guy asked.

"In southwest Denton County," Charlie Delano explained. "It's owned by a feller name o' T. J. Grogan."

"I know Grogan," Guy said. "The last time I heard, he was rustling cattle down around Reynosa. He always liked to keep moving. How's come he's got a ranch now?"

"I think he's prob'ly got backing from Erickson," Charlie said. "But I don't know for sure. At any rate, he's still knowed to use a running iron when it suits him."

"I been meaning to ask," Gideon Magee said. "Just how many is in this here gang?"

"I figger a dozen from what I been told," Charlie said. "But Erickson can hire more pistoleros if he's ever of a mind."

Gideon did some quick figuring. "That's about four of 'em for each of us to start out with."

"Only for a while, I'll bet!" Tyrone exclaimed.

"No matter, they're good boys," Charlie said. "I hate to say it, but it's God's truth. Erickson pays top dollar and he's got top guns."

"I'm a practical son of a bitch," Gideon said. "Why don't we grab a few more Rangers? If nothing else, we can use 'em for backups."

Captain Charlie Delano shook his head. "This here is something I don't want to drag no more'n I have to into. And if there's too many of us, then any sneaky, underhanded stuff we do is gonna come out in the open. The governor don't want that. He'll leave us high and dry."

"I could use another drink," Gideon said.

Charlie turned and signaled the waiter. "Got some dry fellers here."

The man came over. "What'll it be, gents? More o' the same?"

"Bring us a bottle," Charlie said. "Any Kentucky bourbon you got."

The trio of lawmen made small talk until they were served again. Charlie poured out generous glassfuls of the liquor. "Drink up, boys."

Gideon Magee swallowed his rapidly. He sat the glass down. "Now let me get this straight. We're gonna go after a big gang o' murdering thieves that's run by some son of a bitch that's got high connections through a fast-talking lawyer. And we're expected to bend or break the law or anything else it takes to get 'em. And this Erickson and his bunch are so well-placed that if we get caught, there ain't a politician in Texas that'll come out and back us up."

"That's right," Charlie Delano said. "Do you agree to that?"

"Do you two?" Gideon asked.

"Sure," Guy said.

Gideon poured himself another drink. He raised the glass. "Here's to three o' the bravest men in Texas."

"Or the dumbest," Guy Tyrone added with a chuckle.

"Who might end up the deadest," Guy added.

Gideon Magee grinned. "Hell! I'll drink to anything."

Five

A gentle breeze wafted across the top of the hill, barely stirring the bushes that hid Guy Tyrone. He studied the ramshackle ranch house through his field glasses, making careful mental notes of the activity around the place.

A large corral and a barn, which appeared to be constructed better than the house, made up the layout. It was easy for Guy to see that the place was designed to accommodate quite a few residents or visitors. But only five horses stood idly in the corral that could have held three times that many.

Guy, feeling a twinge in his back, stretched a little to get the kinks out. He, Captain Charlie Delano, and Gideon Magee had taken a circuitous route from Dallas out into Denton County. The trip took them four days of continuous riding with only brief stops and early morning starts. They hadn't taken much time to eat, either. The young man was tired, cross, and hungry. Now he and his companions were spread out around T. J. Grogan's ranch to do a couple of hours of observation.

Guy pulled his pocket watch from his vest.

"Damn!" Another half hour was left to go until the return to the rendezvous point to meet up with Charlie and Gideon. Tense and irritable, he went back to spying.

The five men staying at the place moved around only a bit. A couple tended to feeding the horses while a third watered them. They went back in the house and another came out to sit outside on a rickety chair. He stared off in space, then whittled a bit. The fifth man finally joined him and they chatted awhile. Then they went inside to join the other three.

Guy recognized three of them. His patchy career of moving in and out of the law had garnered him a few questionable companions and acquaintances.

He checked his watch again. Another fifteen minutes to go. He continued watching, but everyone stayed inside. The time dragged on and on, it seemed to Guy. But the two hours came to a close. Feeling better, he left the bushes and walked down the far side of the hill where his horse was tied to a tree. He mounted up and rode back toward the wooded bend in the creek where Charlie had instructed them to meet.

When Guy arrived at the spot he found Charlie waiting. The Ranger captain looked up from where he was filling his canteen. "Gideon oughta be here directly," he said.

Guy hobbled his horse next to Charlie's, then sat down beside him on the bank. "I always liked this part o' the country," he remarked.

"Yeah," Charlie agreed. "I reckon I'll settle on a homestead around here sometime when I grow too old to pack a star."

"You gonna farm, Charlie?" Guy asked.

"Hell, no! I'm gonna sit on my wrinkled old ass and drink Kentucky bourbon ever' day 'til I fall off my rocking chair," Charlie said.

Guy chuckled. "That sounds nice. But the onliest way I'll quit is if they shoot me dead."

"Maybe they'll shoot your leg off and you can use that billy club o' yours for a pegleg," Charlie said.

Gideon Magee interrupted them by coming through the brush. He reined in and slipped out of the saddle. "Looks like you two worked a little faster'n me," he greeted the other two.

"Howdy, Gideon," Guy said. "Did you enjoy watching that ranch house?"

"I was just doing something like that in the Cherokee Nation a while back," he remarked. "I had three fellers in an old shack at the bottom of a draw. O' course I was all alone. That's the way us marshals have to work out o' Judge Parker's court."

"Just the same, I bet them owlhoots never saw the sun set on that day, Gideon," Guy remarked.

"You're right about that," Gideon said.

"Did you two see anybody you knowed down there?" Charlie asked.

"I know three," Guy said. "T. J. Grogan, Ned Williams, and Jack Blunt. All of 'em are real mean cusses."

"One of 'em was Ozzie Young," Gideon said. "He's in good comp'ny 'cause he'll shoot another feller on a bet."

"And I know T.J. and the last man Bob Orley," Charlie said. "Orley ain't the friendly sort. And all that adds up to the fact that we ain't gonna be able to sashay in there and casually ask questions.

Any one or two of 'em is gonna know we're lawmen and would be happy as hogs in shit to put bullets in us."

"Do you reckon they're all part o' Ace Erickson's gang?" Guy asked.

"Naw," Charlie said. "I know they ain't. Them boys stay permanent on the ranch. They prob'ly rustle cattle for T.J."

"Then we'd better make any moves we're planning on damn quick," Gideon said. "If Erickson's men show up, that'll mean even more of the meanest bastards in Texas is gonna be down there."

Guy looked at Charlie. "What're we gonna do, Charlie?"

"Well," Charlie said slowly, "I been thinking on that. We're gonna have to move in on them boys and see what they can tell us about Erickson and his gang."

"What makes you think they know anything, Charlie?" Guy asked.

"You can bet that Erickson's men talk plenty while they're hanging around between jobs," Charlie said. "T.J. and them pistoleros of his hear a lot about what they're doing."

"From the way you're talking, I reckon we're gonna have to get one or two of 'em alive, ain't we?" Gideon remarked.

"Can't be helped," Charlie said.

"That makes it more dangerous," Guy said.

"Yeah," Gideon chimed in. "I don't like the idea of raising my fire on any o' them down there."

"Boys, we're in a predicament," Charlie explained. "If we shoot them five, we could lay an ambush for Erickson's gang. But we'd never be able to shoot 'em all up when they showed up.

And we wouldn't know where they were headed or gonna do."

Guy shook his head. "Do you really have any kind o' plan, Charlie?"

"Let me lay it all out," Charlie said. "I want to get what information we can outta Grogan and his boys. Then I want to make a coupla moves against Erickson's men just to keep 'em nervous. That way we can learn all the ins and outs of what they do and where they go to hide."

Gideon pulled his pipe out of his vest. "I still don't get it, Charlie." He got a pouch of tobacco and emptied the right amount into the bowl. "How is hitting 'em gonna help us learn anything?"

"Because one of us is gonna move in and join the gang," Charlie announced.

Gideon shrugged. "Hell, I can't do that. I'm knowed as a lawman. Particular as a U.S. deputy marshal."

Charlie nodded. "And I'm knowed as a Texas Ranger."

Guy listened for the conversation to continue. Then he noticed them both staring at him. At first he was confused. But after a minute, he exclaimed. "Hey!"

"That's right," Charlie said. "I want you to join the gang."

"Good idea," Gideon said. "Guy's been bouncing around on both sides of the law. Nobody knows for sure if he's packing a star or not."

"And when he does, it's always in some town," Charlie said. "He's never been a Ranger or U.S. marshal before."

"Sure," Gideon said. "Even if he run into some feller he throwed in jail, they wouldn't be suspicious. They'd just figger he wandered off the straight and narrow again."

Guy nervously scratched his chin. "Just what the hell's going on?"

"It's real simple," Charlie said. "All you gotta do is join the gang and keep in touch with us to let us know what's going on. Little by little, we'll whittle away at 'em until it's time for a big move against Ace Erickson in Stavanger."

"I ain't real fond o' riding the owlhoot trail," Guy protested. "You don't eat good and don't change clothes too often."

"You don't change much now," Gideon pointed out.

"At least I can when I want to!" Guy snapped.

"You'll be moving around all over the countryside and we'll be following," Charlie explained. "You can send telegraphs to the Windsor Hotel telling us the gang's plans. My contact there knows how to get ahold of me. And we'll pick out some places where you can leave messages under rocks or in trees or anywhere else if you can't get to a telegraph office." He pointed to a large cottonwood nearby. "See that rock at the base o' that tree? You can even stick notes to us in there. We'll camp a ways to the north."

"You're lucky I can write," Guy said sullenly.

"Well, we still got to take T. J. Grogan and his boys to find out the ins and outs of their setup," Charlie said. "I can't let Guy just go on down there and throw in with 'em if we don't have any information to make plans on."

"What do you want us to do, Charlie?" Gideon asked.

"Let Guy ride on down there," Charlie said.

"You and me will come in from the other side." He turned to Guy. "Guy, you get them fellers outside as quick as you can."

"How?" Guy demanded to know.

"Pick a fight with one of 'em," Gideon suggested. "That shouldn't be hard."

"Yeah," Guy agreed. "Me and Jack Blunt don't get along. Fact is, he owes me some money from a card game."

"There it is," Charlie said. "You can start a ruckus over that."

"How soon do you want me to go in there?" Guy asked.

"Right now," Charlie said. "I'd like to get this all over with before dark."

Guy stood up. He sighed, "For God's sake!" Then he shrugged. "What the hell? I'll be looking for you boys about the time me and Jack go outside to settle up on that money."

"Sure," Charlie said. "We'll see you soon."

Guy walked to his horse and raised himself up into the saddle. He pulled the Texas Ranger badge out of his vest pocket and tossed it to Charlie. "I'd feel real dumb if that fell out during the fight."

"You wouldn't feel dumb long," Gideon said. "They'd plug you quick."

Guy only waved as he rode away from the creek and headed for the ranch house. He skirted a hill, then went directly toward the rustic building. He approached the place slowly, being careful to keep his hands in full view.

"Hold it!" The voice came from the house.

Guy stopped. "Yeah?" he shouted.

"You got no business here," the voice informed him.

"I'm looking for a place to spend the night," Guy said.

"It's early yet," the man inside informed him.

"I been traveling since sunrise this morning," Guy explained.

A different voice now sounded. "Is that you, Guy Tyrone?"

"Sure is," Guy said, keeping his tone friendly. "Who's that?"

A man stepped outside. "It's me, Jack Blunt."

"Howdy, Jack," Guy said. "It's been a while." He urged his horse into a slow walk toward the house. "Since when are you a ranch hand?"

Blunt laughed. "This ain't no ranch, you jack-ass."

"Can I spend the night?" Guy said, riding up. "I been sleeping under the stars for a while now." He dismounted as another man came out. Guy recognized him. "Howdy, Ned."

Ned Williams nodded without smiling. "Howdy, Guy."

"You fellers don't mind if I just stay 'til morning, do you?" Guy asked.

"Get down and come on in," Blunt invited.

"I'm obliged," Guy said. He dismounted and led his horse up to the hitching rail. He wrapped the reins around it, and followed the two men into the house.

T. J. Grogan looked at him. "Well, I ain't seen you in a spell."

"Howdy, T.J.," Guy said.

Grogan asked, "What're you up to, Guy?"

"Just moving around," Guy said with a grin. "I got a little problem that keeps me on the dodge."

"Warrants following you around?" Grogan inquired.

"Sure. But it's better'n having some paper 'stead of a lawman after me," Guy said. He knew he had to waste some time to give Charlie and Gideon a chance to move in on the house. "What're all you fellers doing here?"

"Keeping a running iron hot," Jack Blunt said, laughing.

"You ain't never been a cowboy, have you, Guy?" Grogan asked.

"I don't like that kind o' work," Guy said.

"Too bad," Grogan said. "We could use another hand in our operation here."

"Are you rustling, T.J.?" Guy asked.

"Naw!" Williams said with a loud laugh. "We borry 'em, then forget where we got 'em. So we put on our own brand and get on with it."

"I ain't looking for work," Guy said.

"This here's Ozzie Young and Bob Orley," Williams said, introducing the two men Guy didn't know. He pointed to Guy. "This feller works as a town sheriff now and then."

"Howdy," Guy said. He looked at Grogan. "You don't mind me staying 'til morning, do you?"

"Suit yourself," Grogan said.

"I'll unsaddle my horse," Guy said. He went back outside and got the animal, leading it into the corral. As he pulled the saddle off, he glanced around. Finally he spotted Charlie waving at him from the brush. He returned to the house carrying his saddlebags.

"Got anything to throw into the pot for supper?" Blunt asked.

"Sure," Guy said. He steeled himself. "But first.

What about that money you owe me?"

"What money?" Blunt asked.

"Five dollars from that poker game in Balmorhea," Guy said.

Blunt laughed. "Say! That's right." He reached in his pocket and pulled out a gold piece. He flipped it over.

Guy looked at it. It was indeed worth five dollars. He grinned weakly. His plans to start a fight were over before they'd begun. "It looks like we're even."

T. J. Grogan smiled. "Too bad you ain't got no cowboy skills, Guy. You'd have money in your pockets like Jack. You oughta stop being so damned lazy and join up with us. An extry hand would mean extry money."

"I reckon I could use the money, but it ain't worth it to me," Guy said. He thought quickly as he tried to come up with a way to start a ruckus. He said, "Besides, in my book only a low-life son of a bitch rustles cattle."

Grogan laughed. "Ain't that the truth!"

But Bob Orley didn't care for the remark. "Just what do you mean by that?"

Guy knew he had a bite. He had to yank the line hard to reel that particular fish in. "Just what I said, you dumb bastard. Anybody that has to steal cattle to make money is a no-good, turd-eating, lizard-faced donkey. For all the trouble you got to go to, you might as well just sign on as a hand at a ranch somewheres."

All five of the rustlers looked at him with cold, hard faces. Grogan seemed disappointed. "What's got into you, Guy?"

"If you don't like the truth o' what I'm saying,

just get off your asses and step outside. I'll accommodate you," Guy said.

"Are you loco all of a sudden?" Grogan asked.

"Be careful!" Jack Blunt warned the others. "He carries a club on his belt."

"Are you blind too?" Guy asked. "I ain't got my billy with me."

Ned Williams drew his pistol. "I don't know what you're up to. But if you're pulling something, I swear I'll put a bullet in you, Guy Tyrone!"

"You won't be able to shoot him, Ned," Orley said. "On account I'm gonna amuse myself by tom-turkey tromping the shit outta this son of a bitch."

"C'mon, then!" Guy exclaimed. "I never heard son of a bitches that liked to talk so damned much. Let's get this over with." He turned and walked toward the door. He glanced back to see all five following him. Now T. J. Grogan and Jack Blunt also had drawn their irons. Ozzie Young noticed the pistols and did likewise. Guy knew that Charlie and Gideon weren't counting on almost the entire group coming out with their leather cleared.

When he walked through the door, Guy kept moving to get some distance from the house. He turned and made ready to fight. Orley rushed forward.

"Hold it!" Charlie's voice sounded as he stepped from around the house.

The rustlers, armed and mean, whirled around and stared at the unexpected sight.

"Oh, shit!" Charlie said when he noticed the others had pistols in their hands.

Shooting broke out in an instant. Bullets splattered around Charlie. Suddenly appearing with a spitting Colt, Gideon now stepped into view.

Guy drew his pistol with his right hand and fired at almost the same instant, hitting Orley, who had forgotten about fistfighting as he struggled to get his own Colt out for the gunplay.

Now knowing this was some kind of a trap, Williams, Blunt, and Young cut loose in uncoordinated volleys that threw out a swarm of bullets.

But the shots were inaccurate.

Guy had backstepped for more space. He fired in a deliberate cold-blooded manner as did Charlie and Gideon. Within the space of a few explosive seconds, the other three rustlers had joined Bob Orley in death. The four bodies were sprawled close together. T. J. Grogan, dazed by the surprise of the unexpected gunfight, threw down his iron and put up his hands. "I ain't in this!" he cried out.

Guy swung the muzzle of his pistol on him. "We want to talk to you, T.J."

Grogan gave the three lawmen a careful scrutiny. He swung his glare to Guy. "You're packing a star, ain't you?"

"Texas Rangers," Guy said proudly.

"You son of a bitch!" Grogan said, now more mad than scared. "You sneaked in here on us like a damn coyote."

"I kept my purpose to myself, if that's what you mean," Guy admitted.

"I wish you'd make up your mind whether you're gonna be a lawman or not," T.J. complained. "It's hard to see where you stand on things."

Charlie stepped forward. "The only thing you got to worry about is answering a few questions about Ace Erickson's boys that hang out here."

"I don't know what you're talking about," T.J.

mumbled angrily.

"We just killed four cattle-rustling son of a bitches, Grogan," Charlie said. "And if you give us any reason, we'll do the same to you. It'll save us and the state o' Texas a lot o' trouble."

"I want a chance to ride outta here," Grogan said. "Give me your word, Cap'n Delano."

"You got it."

Grogan took a deep breath, then started talking. He told about the arrangements he had with Erickson's gang to stay on his ranch between jobs. Erickson didn't want his boys around Stavanger too much, because they would be linked with him there. He only let them in after they did particularly good jobs.

"And that's where they are right now," Grogan said. "They pulled a big one on a Wells Fargo gold shipment—all twenty-dollar gold pieces—so he let 'em come into Stavanger for a couple o' days."

"When're they due back?" Gideon asked, butting in.

"Tomorry," Grogan answered. "And I ain't planning on being here then." He looked at the three lawmen. "You fellers got to promise to not let Erickson know I told on him. If he ever finds out, he'll send Gustavo Fairweather to gun me down."

"We won't say nothing," Charlie said. "And I'm holding to my word, Grogan. My advice is for you to put as much distance between Denton County and yourself as you can. And keep it that way. Saddle up now and get out."

Grogan needed no second invitations. He rushed inside to get some things, then quickly reappeared to rush over and saddle his horse.

Charlie chuckled. "I see you got your running

iron with you."

"A man's got to make a living no matter where he goes," T.J. said defensively. Within ten minutes he'd galloped away.

"Now what do we do?" Guy asked.

"We bury these four to get 'em outta sight," Charlie said. "Then I gotta do some thinking."

"Are you gonna come up with another plan?" Guy asked hopefully.

"I think the one where you join the gang is gonna work out real good," Charlie said.

"Me too," Gideon added.

Guy displayed a weak grin. "Damn!"

Six

Charlie Delano and Gideon Magee rode as far away from Grogan's ranch as they could while still maintaining contact with Guy Tyrone. They didn't want the younger lawman to be completely isolated and in harm's way all on his own. Meanwhile, the younger man stayed on the small spread to wait for the return of Erickson's men.

Charlie and Gideon went off several miles to the south toward Dallas to set up camp. Once settled in, there was very little they could do but simply wait for things to start happening. With little control over the situation, they had no other choice. However, it was decided that if they didn't hear from Guy within a week they planned to make a careful return to the vicinity of the ranch. If Erickson's gang had gone off on a job with Guy Tyrone, he was to leave a note for them at the base of the cottonwood tree that Charlie had pointed out as a good place to hide messages.

Now, after two days and a couple of nights all by himself on the place, Guy began to feel eerie and uncomfortable. He hated to admit it even to himself, but sleeping in the ranch house alone with the wind whistling and coyotes howling outside made all his superstitions and natural fears leap to life.

Guy didn't know if he believed in ghosts or not, but he was glad that the bodies of the four dead rustlers weren't close-by. Charlie and Gideon had hauled them off to be deeply buried far away, so the corpses wouldn't be discovered by any of Erickson's gang if any wild animals happened to dig them up. At the site of the gunfight in front of the ranch house, the Rangers had even gone to the trouble of giving the ground a good raking and brushing with tree branches to obscure any tracks or places where blood had soaked into the dirt.

By the morning of the third day, Guy was no longer nervous about greeting the bandits. In fact, he looked forward to their arrival at the ranch. Whatever uneasiness he'd felt about meeting them didn't match the nervous agitation of being alone out there in that wind-rattled ranch house situated in the lonely prairie country.

When the gang did finally show up, it was late afternoon and Guy was watering his horse. He looked up and feigned surprise at their arrival. Although he inwardly tensed himself for an unfriendly confrontation, he played the role of a casual visitor to the ranch. The six gave him looks of unabashed curiosity and suspicion as they rode into the yard.

Still in their saddles, they gathered around him by the trough. One of them gave the place a careful look-see, then glared at Guy. It was easy to tell he noted the absence of any other horses except Guy's.

"Where's Grogan?"

"Who's Grogan?" Guy said back to him.

The man dismounted and walked over, leading his horse. "He's the feller that lives here."

"It don't look to me like nobody lives here," Guy said.

"We live here," the man said.

"Then you oughta know where your friend is," Guy said. "You fellers a posse?"

Loud laughter broke out among the group of horsemen.

"Mister, I'd rather be taken for a son of a bitch than a damn lawman," the man said.

"So would I," Guy said. He decided it was time to get things on a friendlier level. "My name is Guy Tyrone. I'm an old friend o' Grogan's. You must be the fellers that bunk here now and again."

"That's us. I'm Ned Paulson."

"Howdy." Guy offered his hand. "Grogan and the fellers got the word on a herd o' horses meant for the army up in the Injun Territory. They said something about looking 'em over."

More laughter broke out.

"When're they coming back?" Paulson asked.

Guy shrugged. "They didn't say. It seemed they had a ways to go, though."

"It must've been a perty good deal to get Grogan off this place," Paulson said.

"Howdy, Guy." One of the men rode forward. "I ain't seen you since we was in the lockup down at Quemado."

Guy felt a twinge of relief. Here was a man he'd been in jail with. "Now there you are, Jess Garbel!"

Garbel dismounted and walked over to shake hands. "It's been a coupla years, ain't it?" He turned to Paulson. "This here's a good feller to have around in a fight. And we got into 'em at Quemado, that's for sure." He chuckled. "Still got that billy club?"

Guy shook his head. "No. I misplaced it somewheres, I guess. It ain't worth much."

"It was real hard wood, wasn't it?" Garbel asked.

Guy grinned. "Sure thing. Jirara wood. The hardest wood knowed to man."

"He knocked out a sheriff and two deputies down there," Garbel said. "He was swinging that damn billy club so loco-like that they had to get a crowd to drag his ass off to jail."

"I was in there for what? Sixty? Ninety days?" Guy mused. "Hell, I don't remember now."

"Where you headed, Guy?" Garbel asked.

"No place in particular," Guy said. "Grogan wanted me to go with him, but I ain't much into stealing horses or cattle. It's too much like work."

Paulson was interested. "Maybe we can offer you something you'd like better."

"Sure," Guy said. "What kind o' line are you fellers in?"

"Didn't Grogan tell you?" Paulson asked.

"Nope," Guy answered. "As a matter o' fact, Grogan seemed kind o' nervous when it come to talking about his boarders. So I didn't press it. I got to thinking that maybe he owed you fellers some money or something."

"Naw," Paulson said. "We ain't mad at Grogan."

"Then, if you don't mind telling me, what's your game?" Guy asked.

"We pull special jobs," Paulson said. "Like trains and banks mostly."

"I bet there's more money in that than in stealing horses," Guy said.

"I bet there is too," Garbel said with a laugh.

"Anyhow, what's so special about 'em?" Guy asked.

"We get inside information on the where and the when to do it," Garbel said. "I think it'd suit you fine."

"I'm short o' cash money," Guy said.

"Then why don't you stick around with us for a while?" Paulson said. "We'll prob'ly be going out on a job pretty soon."

"What kind o' job?" Guy asked.

"It depends on what they give us," Paulson explained. "We never know in advance."

By then all the other men were dismounting and leading their horses into the corral. Paulson motioned Guy to follow as he took care of his own mount. "We got direction."

"Direction? What're you talking about?" Guy asked, walking alongside him.

"Never mind that," Paulson said. "But we hear about good places and times to make money. And we follow up on it. Still inter'sted?"

"Damn right," Guy said.

"Well, we'll all settle in here and you can meet the rest o' the boys," Paulson said. "See anybody else you know?"

Guy studied the other four men pulling saddles off their horses. "I don't think so."

"Well, you'll know 'em soon enough," Garbel said.

Guy walked to the ranch house between Paulson and Garbel. They were followed by the rest of the gang. When the group went inside, everybody settled in to stay a bit. In a way it was nice to have company, even if it was a bunch of men who would shoot him like a dog if they ever discovered the truth about him.

Jess Garbel did the honors of making introductions. Guy met Shorty Darnell, Willy Kemp, Lee Fenney, and Elmer Sherman. Convinced that Guy was to be trusted because Garbel had told them of being in jail with him, they accepted him. But it wasn't done with a lot of friendliness. In their line of business, a new man had to prove himself before he could really become a part of the group.

"I got a pot o' coffee going in the fireplace," Guy announced. "You fellers just help yourselves."

They wordlessly retrieved tin cups from their belongings and trooped over to the boiling brew. They drained the pot.

"I'll make some more," Guy said.

"Bring your poke o' coffee over here," Garbel said. "I'll pour some of mine in to add to it."

"Sure," Guy said. He took the cloth sack of coffee over and let the outlaw pour some of his own. Then he went to the fire and fixed another potful from the bucket he'd kept filled with well water.

Ned Paulson joined him. "The only thing better'n coffee is whiskey."

"I know something better," Willy Kemp said from where he worked at spreading out his bedroll. "And we left it back there in Stavanger."

"Don't you go thinking on that taste o' women we enjoyed these past two nights," Paulson said. "You'll go crazy."

"No, I won't," Kemp said. "I'll go back to Stavanger."

"Not with Ace Erickson there," Lee Fenney warned him.

Guy saw a chance. "Who's Ace Erickson?" he

asked in as innocent a tone as he could muster.

"You'll find out someday," Garbel said.

"And again, maybe you won't," Kemp added.

"Sounds like it's none o' my business," Guy remarked.

"That's right," Kemp said. "It's none o' your damn business."

"Now ain't that just what I said?" Guy asked in a cold voice.

"I'm just making sure you understand it," Kemp said.

"You sound as if you like to teach lessons," Guy said.

Everyone in the room stopped what they were doing and turned to see where that particular conversation was going to go.

Kemp stood up from straightening out his blankets. "Yeah. I teach lessons good."

Guy faced him squarely. He sensed he was about to go through an impromptu test. It was important how he handled the situation. Any hesitation or show of weakness on his part could prove a mite more than embarrassing. It could be fatal. He steeled himself and said, "You're talking strong like you want to teach me something."

"Maybe I do," Kemp said.

"Get on with it, then," Guy invited him.

Kemp walked toward him slowly, clenching and unclenching his fists. He was shorter than Guy, but heavier and more muscular. His shoulders tensed as he closed in. Suddenly he rushed forward and swung a roundhouse punch.

Guy ducked under it, coming up with a whiplike uppercut that connected solidly with Kemp's jaw.

Kemp staggered back, blinking his eyes. After shaking his head a couple of times, he charged again.

Guy let him have a good one on the left side of his head, then drove a straight punch into Kemp's nose. He could feel the organ crunch under the blow.

Kemp, blood dripping freely from his nostrils, only shook his head again. He made another attempt.

Guy slammed him twice more, then gave a backhand punch that almost turned his opponent around. Three more quick but hard punches sent Kemp to the dirt floor.

Garbel laughed. "Hey, Willy, you better be glad he ain't got that billy club of his with him. He's doing you bad enough with his fists."

Kemp got to his feet and wiped at his nose. "I reckon the fight's over," he said.

"Fine by me," Guy said.

Kemp went back to his bedroll to nurse his hurts.

Paulson, as gang leader, spoke loud and clear. "I don't want this to go no farther, understand?" He looked at them. "Goddamn it! I mean what I say. If you want to fight, then do it in the open. The first man that brings a gun or knife—" He glared at Guy. "—or billy club into the thing gets lead poisoning. That's my word on it."

"I ain't mad," Guy said. "And I ain't got that billy club with me, like I said."

"I ain't riled neither," Kemp said, looking up from blotting at his nose. "I just wanted to see what kind o' feller he was."

"Well, do you know?"

"I reckon," Kemp said.

"I'll finish making the coffee," Guy said. He turned to the task.

Garbel squatted down by the fireplace to watch. "You done good, Guy," he said in a low whisper. "But I knowed you would."

"That Kemp can't fight for shit," Guy whispered back.

Garbel chuckled. "We've all whipped his ass at least a coupla times. The dumb son of a bitch just can't get in and give a lick no matter how hard he tries." Then he said, "But he's the best shot in the gang. So don't go drawing on him. Just foller Ned Paulson's orders."

"That I'll do," Guy said. He went about the task of brewing the coffee. Now and then he glanced over toward Willy Kemp, but the man seemed satisfied the incident was over. He finished spreading out his bedroll, then lay down on it. Guy waited until the coffee was done, then poured out a cup. He walked over to Kemp. "Here you go."

Kemp looked up at him. He sensed Guy was making an offer of friendship. He decided to take it. "Thanks." He took the coffee and started drinking without any further comment.

Guy went back to the fireplace where the others now served themselves. "How'd I do with the coffee, boys?"

"Hot and strong," Ned Paulson said.

"That's the way I always make it," Guy said.

Paulson drank deeply. "I want lookouts posted afore dark, boys. "Shorty, you're first. Then Willy, Elmer, Jess, and Lee."

"I'll pull a turn," Guy volunteered.

Paulson shook his head. "Not yet, Tyrone. We'll

season you a little to see just how trustworthy you are.

"I reckon that's smart," Guy allowed.

The men continued settling back into the crude ranch house. Another hour passed and they were all hungry. Rather than prepare their supper communally, the gang cooked the food individually in the fireplace. Then all went over to a table in the corner to sit down and eat. The shadows began to lengthen considerably by the time Paulson ordered the first guard out.

Shorty Darnell, taking his carbine, left the house. Guy watched him go, then settled down on his bedroll. The rest of the gang began their evening routine. Lee Fenney took out a harmonica and began playing softly to himself with surprisingly pleasing results. Willy Kemp, his nose battered but recovering, went to sleep. Ned Paulson went outside to walk around for a spell.

"Hey, Guy," Jess Garbel said. "You want to play cards with me and Elmer?"

"What're you playing?" Guy asked.

"If you'll sit in, we'll try some poker," Garbel said.

"Sure," Guy said. He got up and joined them at the table.

The cards had just been shuffled and cut when Paulson came through the door. "Rider coming!"

Everyone jumped to life, grabbing their carbines and rushing to various windows. Guy stood there for a moment watching.

"Tyrone," Paulson said. "Take the window on the south."

"Sure." He got his Winchester and went to the post.

Paulson glanced out. "Relax, boys. It's Gustavo."

A horse coming to a halt could be heard outside. Moments later the door opened and Gustavo Fairweather walked into the place. He glanced around. "Where the hell is Grogan?"

"Him and his boys took off," Paulson said. "They got wind of easy pickings on a herd o' horses." He pointed to Guy. "That feller stayed on."

Fairweather glared at Guy. "Who are you?"

"My name is Guy Tyrone," Guy said. He took careful note of the newcomer. Both Charlie Delano and Gideon Magee had spoken of him in respectful tones. "You're packing a star, ain't you?"

"That's not for you to fret about," Fairweather said.

"Guy and me was in jail together in Quemado," Garbel said.

That made Fairweather relax. "Howdy."

"Howdy," Guy said.

"I'm gonna give him a try," Paulson said.

"Well, he's gonna get a chance to show what he can do real quick," Fairweather said. "There's a stage out o' Lubbock just ripe for the picking."

Paulson nodded. "Yeah. Ace told me about it when we was in Stavanger."

"You'll be able to hit it just north o' Littlefield about noon a coupla days from now," Fairweather said. "They're carrying a strongbox o' greenbacks stuck under the front seat. Only one guard with the driver. Wells Fargo didn't want to call attention to the load."

"How about that driver and guard?" Paulson asked.

"They're strictly Wells Fargo men, so be damn

careful," Fairweather warned him.

"Anything else worth taking?" Paulson asked.

"Nope," Fairweather said. "Just get under that front seat. It's a cattle association funds that's supposed to be used to lease some land up in the Injun Territory. Should be about twenty-five thousand dollars."

"We'll be there," Paulson said. "We'll leave in the morning."

"And I'll see you in Stavanger in about three days, then," Fairweather said. He gave Guy another glance, then left with the same abruptness that marked his arrival.

Garbel chuckled, and reached over to give Guy a friendly slap on the shoulder. "Well! By God, it looks like you'll have money pretty damn quick now."

Guy grinned. "That's good." Then he asked, "Has anybody got any whiskey?"

He figured that being a Texas Ranger and riding the owlhoot trail at the same time was enough to drive anybody to drink.

Seven

Guy Tyrone squatted in the shade of the oak tree, hanging on to his horse's reins with one hand and slapping at flies with the other. Bored, yet uneasy, he glanced occasionally at his companions nearby.

He and the members of the Ace Erickson gang had been waiting along the road three miles north of the town of Littlefield for more than four hours. The other six men, with the exception of Willy Kemp on watch, lounged around the area showing their impatience now and then with scratching, spitting, and an occasional curse.

"The son of a bitch is late," Lee Fenney remarked.

"No shit?" Shorty Darnell said. "Did you figger that out all on your own?"

"How come ever' time I say something, you got a smart-ass remark?" Fenney asked.

"Things you say is dumb," Darnell told him.

"Oh, yeah?"

"Shut up," Ned Paulson said. "It's bad enough having to wait without listening to a coupla shitheads carry on."

The pair quieted down again.

Guy hadn't had a chance to leave any sort of message for Charlie Delano and Gideon Magee before they all left Grogan's ranch. If they went to the cottonwood tree to look under the rock, the only thing they'd find would be bugs—or maybe a snake.

The gang had kept a close eye on Guy and he didn't want to do anything to raise their suspicions, so he kept himself close to the ranch house right up to the time they galloped off to pull the stagecoach job.

"Is Ace gonna let us go back to Stavanger?" Elmer Sherman asked.

Paulson shook his head. "Nope. We had our fun for a while. He'll send us some whiskey and a couple o' Dinah's gals for a celebration, then we'll have to settle down and wait for the next job."

Guy suddenly became interested at the mention of women. He spoke up. "How many did you say is sent?"

"Two," Garbel answered.

"Are they pretty?" Guy asked.

Paulson looked at him and winked. "You want pretty or you want willing?"

"They must be ugly as one-eared mules," Guy said.

Shorty Darnell laughed. "Don't go insulting one-eared mules."

"What kind o' gals is gonna put up with going out on a ranch for three or four days with a bunch o' trail-dirty, drunk men?" Garbel said. "There ain't no beauties that'll be desperate enough to do that. If they won't go out to Grogan's, they get fired or beat up."

"They get both," Darnell said.

"Maybe I'll wait 'til we can get into town," Guy said. He could become starved for female companionship, but there was a limit to what he would accept no matter what the conditions.

Fenney laughed. "After you been out to Grogan's for three or four months, they'll look pretty enough. Don't you worry none about that."

A sharp whistle broke into the conversation.

"That's Willy!" Sherman said.

A moment later, Willy Kemp appeared from the brush. "Stage is on the way."

"A driver and guard only?" Paulson asked.

"That's all I seen," Kemp said. "Looked like passengers inside. But could be guards there too."

"Could be," Paulson agreed. "But Gustavo said it was an easy deal. In any case, let's take care just the same." He pointed to Darnell and Sherman. "You two mount up and get on the road to stop 'em. And keep close eyes on the pair on the wagon seat." He gestured to Kemp and Fenney. "Stay afoot and take the right side. Me and Jess and Guy will do the same on the left. We'll pull the money out." He pulled his bandanna up. "Guy, I want you to watch careful how we operate. This is your first time, so's you can learn something too. But be ready to jump in if something happens."

"Sure, Ned," Guy said.

Paulson said, "Let's go, boys!"

The others also made sure their faces were covered as they followed the gang leader down toward the road to get into position for the robbery.

Almost fifteen minutes passed before the sound of the stage could be heard. The racket was a combination of pounding hooves, clanging, clacking, bumping, and creaking.

Garbel laughed. "The son of a bitch don't exactly sneak up on you, does he?"

"Still not as noisy as a train," Kemp observed.

"Shut up!" Paulson nervously ordered again. "And be ready for trouble. You dumb bastards don't seem to realize that if something goes wrong, you'll be laying dead on this road."

Now the seriousness of the situation really dawned on Guy Tyrone. If he were killed or captured, as far as the law was concerned he was a desperado. The governor of Texas had said he wouldn't back them up if something went wrong. He silently damned Captain Charlie Delano to hell as he waited.

On the other hand, he admitted to himself, he could certainly use the money.

The stage came into view through an arch of trees that spanned the road. Both Shorty Darnell and Elmer Sherman went into action. They galloped forward, shooting into the air.

"Hold on!" Darnell yelled.

"Stop or die, goddamn you!" Sherman added.

Now the rest of the gang jumped into the action, splitting off to the sides of the vehicle they had been assigned by Ned Paulson. All fired a couple of shots to punctuate the orders that had been shouted.

"Whoa!"

The driver pulled back on the reins while the guard raised his hands, opening and closing them to emphasize he had no concealed weapon with him. The stage camc to a halt as the horses reacted to the driver's actions and shouted commands.

The guard looked down at the seven bandits. "What the hell are you fellers doing? We ain't got nothing worth this trouble. Just some folks inside. And they ain't rich."

Paulson glared at him. "Now you're a lying son of a bitch, ain't you?" He motioned to the passengers. "Ever'body outside!"

Four very frightened traveling people—three men and a middle-aged woman—climbed out and walked over to the side of the road keeping their hands up.

"You can lower your hands if you want, ma'am," Guy said as gallantly as he could.

She smiled uncertainly and slowly brought them down to her side. The woman spoke in an uneasy voice. "Thank you, sir. Thank you most kindly."

"You can be nice to the lady, but keep them others covered," Paulson said. He leaped inside the stage and sat down on the back seat. Bracing himself, he kicked at the base of the opposite seat. The wood splintered and cracked as it gave way under the heavy pounding. Paulson leaned down and reached inside. He pulled out a large leather bag with a heavy padlock. "I got it!"

Guy watched as the gang chief leaped to the ground. He threw the satchel down and fired a couple of shots at the lock until it split apart and the hasp opened.

The guard looked at the driver. "Damn! He knowed exactly where to find it."

The driver shrugged. "I reckon."

"This job ain't what it used to be," the guard complained.

"You're right about that," the driver agreed.

Paulson checked the interior of the satchel. "Yep! Just what we're looking for." He motioned to the passengers. "Get inside, folks. We don't want your wallets and watches. You can go on your way now."

Guy helped the lady up the step, then closed the door. "Y'all have a nice trip, hear?"

Paulson gestured with his pistol at the driver. "What the hell are you waiting for?"

"Not a damn thing, mister!" the man said. He slapped the reins and the stage was pulled away by the horses.

The gang waited for the vehicle to roll out of sight and sound. Paulson said, "C'mon, Shorty. You and me are going to Stavanger."

"Sure, Ned," Shorty Darnell said happily.

"Lemme go, Ned!" Kemp asked.

"Shut up!" Paulson ordered him. "The rest o' you get back to Grogan's and wait. Me and Shorty will be back with your cuts in a coupla days."

Within moments the entire group was mounted and heading for their destinations. Guy rode beside Jess Garbel, keeping his horse at an easy pace with the others as they headed back to Denton County.

"Hey!" Guy shouted. "Ain't you fellers worried about a posse? When that stage reaches Mule Shoe, they're gonna let folks know about the robbery."

"Don't worry none, Guy," Jess yelled back. "Once we're across the Denton line, we come under the jurisdiction of Sheriff Gustavo Fairweather. I don't think he'll try real hard to find us, do you?"

Guy laughed. "I reckon not."

They rode on in a good mood. All knew they would soon have some cash money in their pockets to enjoy themselves for a spell. It was true that they'd be holed up at Grogan's for a while, but in a few weeks Ace Erickson would set things up for them in Stavanger and they could have a good time drinking, dallying with Dinah's girls, and gambling.

It took most of the rest of that day to get back to their headquarters. As they came over the crest of the rise leading down into the ranch, Lee Fenney raised his hand and signaled a halt. When Ned Paulson was gone, he was in charge.

Willy Kemp asked, "How's come you stopped us, Lee?" His voice had a slight nasal tone to it due to the swelling he still had from being punched around by Guy Tyrone.

"The place is dark," Lee said. "That means Grogan and his boys ain't back. There could be some starpackers down there waiting for us." He pointed to Kemp and Sherman. "You boys go around to the west. Jess and Guy take the east. I'll go down straight ahead. Once you're close in, dismount and go on foot. Now be careful!"

"I thought Gustavo Fairweather kept things safe here in Denton County," Guy said.

"He can't be ever' place at once," Fenney said.

"Yeah," Garbel said. "Some U.S. marshals or Texas Rangers might have snuck in there."

Guy hoped that Charlie Delano and Gideon Magee hadn't done anything foolish like decide to spring an ambush. In the darkness they wouldn't stand the chance of a mouse in a snake hole.

Fenney shouted, "Move out, boys, and try not to sound like a herd o' stampeding buffalo."

They rode forward at a walk with drawn guns. The going was slow for the first hundred yards, then came to a halt when they dismounted.

"Hold our horses, Guy," Jess said.

Guy took the reins and led the animals around to the cover of a stand of trees. Then he waited, keeping on the alert to make sure nobody sneaked up on him in the dark.

A few minutes later, Fenney's voice sounded from the ranch house. "Come on in, boys, it's all clear!"

Guy walked on down to the place and found Garbel waiting for him. He gave his outlaw friend back his horse and the two went to the corral to unsaddle, feed, and water their mounts.

"Are we just gonna sit around here?" Guy asked.

"Sure," Garbel replied. "At least 'til we hear about another job. Then we'll go pull it and come on back for a spell. After a while, if we done real good, we'll have a good ol' time there in Stavanger."

"Are all the jobs as easy as this one?" Guy inquired as he led his horse over to the grain trough. "I don't think none of us worked up a sweat."

"We get trouble sometimes," Garbel said, doing as Guy had done with his own animal. "We hit this here train and ol' Shorty Darnell almost got shot by a guard. But Lee Fenney got the son of a bitch first."

"That driver and guard sure was surprised we knowed where the loot was," Guy said.

The two left their mounts eating as they walked back to the house. "Maybe they was and maybe they wasn't," Garbel said. "It might've been one o' them that tipped off Ace Erickson about where the money would be."

"You don't know who the inside man is?" Guy asked.

"We sure as hell don't," Garbel said. "Ace sure ain't gonna tell us. That'd be pretty dumb of him to let ever' one in on his secrets." He frowned.

"Hey, how come you're asking so damn many questions?"

Guy thought fast. "Well, hell, a feller is gonna be curious about a setup like this, ain't he? I never heard tell nothing like it before. I mean, that was sweeter picking than an unwatched melon patch."

"Sure it was, but if I was you I'd keep my mouth shut when it comes to asking too many questions," Garbel counseled him. "It ain't real smart to be nosy in this outfit."

"I'll remember that," Guy said.

The two went into the house and found the others cooking a rare communal supper. Most of the time they seemed to prefer to tend to their own vittles. They had pooled together all their beans and biscuits.

Garbel shook his head in disapproval. "That ain't fit eating, boys. We got to do some hunting tomorrow, boys. We can't go long without meat."

"I'll go," Guy volunteered. "I'll get up early in the morning."

"Good idea," Fenney said. "Jess and Elmer can go with you."

"Sure," Guy said. "I'll be glad to have the company." He'd hoped to go alone to try to either look up Charlie and Gideon or at least leave them a note.

"You make good coffee, Guy," Fenney said. "Why don't you do that while me and Willy cook?"

"Sure," Guy said. "That seems like a good tradeoff." He went to his bedroll and other possessions to get the pot. "Ever'thing is teamwork around here, ain't it?"

"Yeah," Fenney said. "And shame on the son of a bitch who goes against the group."

"Yeah," Elmer Sherman said. "It ain't real healthy."

"By God, I'll bet it ain't," Guy said, and walked over to the fire to start the coffee.

Eight

Guy Tyrone's cut out of the stage robbery amounted to an even one thousand dollars.

He had never had that much money in his life. As he counted the cash over and over, the lawman experienced a few short doubts about whether packing a star was worth all the effort or not. He knew that even Captain Charlie Delano wasn't paid wages like that in the Texas Rangers.

The other members of the gang got a little bit more, but that only because they were more experienced and had proven themselves over several robberies. But Ned Paulson assured Guy he would get an equal amount in the future.

"You done good, Guy," Paulson said. "You handled yourself like a natural."

Guy smiled weakly. "Thanks, Ned." He really didn't know whether to consider the statement a compliment or not.

Paulson and Shorty Darnell had returned to the ranch two days following the armed theft. No one was certain what the entire take had been or what Ace Erickson had grabbed for himself and his lawyer pal Maxwell Banter. The gang contented itself with the knowledge that at least some of the money had to go to buy information on upcoming jobs, which created some expenses not normally encountered in run-of-the mill outlawry. As long as the money kept coming in steady and plentiful, none would be inclined to complain about the arrangements of sharing the booty.

The immediate results of divvying up the loot was a big poker game that got going right away. The men gathered around the largest table in the ranch house, setting out the several bottles of whiskey that Paulson and Darnell had brought back with them from Stavanger. After a couple of preliminary swigs of the liquor, the outlaws began the game with a faded, greasy deck of cards.

Guy didn't take part in the game. He was never good at gambling since he didn't have the concentration to keep track of what was going on. But, because there was nothing much better to do, Guy stood around and watched for a while.

"Say, fellers," he finally said as the tenth hand was being dealt out. "Wasn't we talking about going hunting? I'm tired o' biscuits and beans."

"We'll get to it directly," Paulson said, picking up five cards for a game of draw. He scowled across the table at Shorty Darnell. "Did you deal this mess?"

Darnell grinned. "I sure as hell did."

"Some nice elk or even rabbit'd taste good," Guy said.

The men around the table turned in cards to trade for others in order to build better hands. They paid no attention to the speaker.

"I'll bet five dollars," Elmer Sherman said.

He was raised, that raise raised, and finally everyone around the table had put in to make the pot right. Willy Kemp, the last man to bet, showed a full house. The others groaned as he swept the money in toward his side of the table.

"Maybe them gals would like some meat too when they get here," Guy suggested. "It'd put 'em in a friendlier mood if we had some good grub to give 'em."

Ned Paulson turned and glared at him. "God-damn it, Guy! If you want to go hunting, go on ahead and leave us in peace! Better you bother a deer or a rabbit than honest poker players!"

That was exactly what Guy wanted to do. But he didn't want to arouse suspicion by appearing too anxious. He kept his eagerness under control and acted nonchalant. "Say, would any o' you fellers like to come along?" he asked. "Two can always hunt better'n one."

"Go on," Jess Garbel said as he picked up the cards. "There ain't none of us want to go riding around and hunt. We want to play cards." He immediately turned his attention back to the game. "Seven-toed pete, deuces wild," he called out as he began to shuffle. "Let's all ante up a dollar."

Guy went to his bedroll and picked up his carbine. He walked softly but quickly to the door, eased through it, and stepped outside. He went rapidly to his horse to saddle up and get off the ranch. No more than ten minutes had passed when he rode out of the yard and headed up into the surrounding hills.

The first place he went was to the cottonwood tree that he, Charlie, and Gideon had used for a rendezvous point during their first scout of Grogan's ranch. He carefully searched the ground for signs or tracks left behind by his friends. After a few moments, he figured out they'd probably been there a couple of times to look for notes under the rock selected to hide them. Only someone looking for the signs could have told that the ground had been swept clear of tracks.

Guy rode out of the area, heading south to locate the camp where his partners spent their time holding up and waiting for him. It took Guy less than an hour to pick up the trail he'd been looking for. He made slow progress, retracing his route a couple of times when he found he'd gone off in the wrong direction, but an hour later he could hear a familiar whistle.

Guy whistled back. "Hey!" he added.

"C'mon in," Charlie Delano's voice sounded in the distance.

Guy rode toward it, going down into a small ravine where he eventually spotted Gideon Magee standing back in the brush. Guy nodded to him. "I'm alone."

Gideon led him farther back into the brush until they reached a hidden camp. Charlie Delano squatted there drinking a cup of coffee. The Ranger captain nodded to him. "Howdy, Guy."

"Howdy, Charlie," Guy said. He dismounted and looked around the comfortable setup. "I hope you two ain't been suffering too much since I went away and left you."

"We been getting by," Gideon said, settling down by the fire. "How've you been?"

"I robbed a stage," Guy said.

"Ain't you a caution," Gideon said with a snort.

Charlie was more interested. "Was that the one north o' Littlefield?"

"Yeah," Guy answered. "How'd you find out about it?"

"I was in Dallas last night," Charlie said. "The

news had been telegraphed in to the governor's office. Pascal Bond told me about it."

"You mean I'm out there up to my neck in desperados and you been going into Dallas?" Guy asked.

"Sure thing," Charlie said.

"Me too," Gideon said. "And staying at the Windsor Hotel."

"You two son of a bitches!" Guy swore.

"Don't stand there cussing," Gideon said. "Tell us about the stagecoach."

"Gustavo Fairweather come into the ranch and told us about it," Guy said. "He even savvied where the money was hid on it. Right under the front seat."

"How'd he know that?" Charlie asked.

Guy shrugged. "When I tried to find out, they told me not to get nosy. It wasn't healthy. I'm inclined to believe 'em."

"Have they asked about Grogan?" Charlie wanted to know.

"Yeah. I told 'em that him and his boys had took off to rob a herd o' horses up in the Injun Territory," Guy explained. "They believed me."

"That's a good story," Gideon said.

"It damn well better be," Guy said.

"Does Gustavo Fairweather always bring instructions on their jobs?" Charlie asked.

"I think so," Guy replied. "And after the job, Ned Paulson and one other feller takes the loot into Stavanger to be divvied up."

"How much did you get?" Gideon asked.

"One thousand Yankee dollars," Guy said with a grin. "And I'm keeping it."

"It's evidence," Charlie reminded him.

But Guy shook his head. "Nope. Dead bandits is evidence. This is *mine!*"

"Good enough," Charlie allowed. "Just remember to try and let us know about the next job so's we can bushwhack the bastards."

"I'll try my best," Guy promised. "But the money does come in handy, believe me."

"You wouldn't mind sharing, would you?" Gideon asked.

"Why? So you can have some spending money when you got to Dallas?" Guy asked. "I ain't giving you nothing."

"Suit yourself, you stingy bastard," Gideon said with more understanding than animosity. "Anyhow, tell us how you got away from the ranch," Gideon requested.

"I told 'em we should go hunting, since all we're eating is biscuits and beans," Guy said. "But they wanted to play poker. I reckon they must do that after ever' job. Anyhow, I kept pestering 'til they damn near made me leave."

"You better go back with some game, then," Charlie said.

"All there is around here are rabbits," Gideon said. "We could help you shoot two or three. If we had more time we could get elk or deer."

"Maybe we'll be lucky," Charlie said. "C'mon. We got to get cracking on this. I don't want Guy away from that bunch for too long."

The three lawmen formed an impromptu hunting team. In order to keep the sound of shots away from Grogan's ranch, they moved farther south. It took three hours of scouring the creek bottoms and rolling hills until they finally flushed a small doe.

"She's mine!" Guy hollered. He reined in and pulled his Winchester from the saddle boot. A quick aim and squeeze on the trigger brought the animal down.

They rode over to it. Gideon shook his head. "She's a small one."

"Enough to feed a few folks at least twice, though," Guy observed. "If you make a stew."

Charlie and Gideon helped Guy tie the dead animal on the back of his saddle. Charlie patted the deer. "At least that'll make it look like you was hunting."

"Damn it, I *was* hunting," Guy pointed out.

"We helped you," Gideon said.

"You didn't do nothing," Guy argued. "I seen the deer—"

"I seen her first," Charlie countered.

"I would've seen her anyhow," Guy said. "And I shot her."

"You get on back there," Gideon said. "It don't matter who did what."

"And don't forget to try to get information to us on the next job," Charlie said. "We want that gang did in like they ran into bad luck or something. Then we can go into Stavanger for the showdown with Ace Erickson."

"Don't forget Gustavo Fairweather," Guy said. "He's the meanest son of a bitch I've ever seen." He grinned. "Outside o' Gideon Magee, that is."

"That's right," Gideon said. "And don't you forget it!"

Charlie looked straight at Guy. "Just remember you're there to trap that gang, not make a lot o' money."

"I know how we could get 'em fast," Guy said. "If I was a backshooter, I could get ever' one of 'em while they was asleep."

"Would you do that?" Gideon asked.

Guy shook his head. "Nope. Not my style. But I'll lead 'em into a trap the first chance I get." He stepped up in the saddle, swinging his leg over the deer as he forked it. "I'm on my way back to the ranch. See you boys later, if I can. Especially if I learn about a job that's gonna be pulled. If I can't get to you, at least I'll leave you a note first chance."

"So long," Charlie said.

"Good luck," Gideon added.

Guy waved and rode off, turning north to rejoin the gang. It took him a couple of hours to get back to the ranch. When he got there he noticed a wagon with a canvas cover in front of the house. A lot of whooping and hollering came from inside. Guy figured the gals must have arrived.

He untied the deer and slung it across his shoulders. When he walked through the door, everyone in the room turned and looked at him. "I told you I was going hunting," Guy said.

"By God, you did!" Ned Paulson said. He walked over a bit drunkenly. "Looks like we got some venison for tomorrow, ain't we?"

"Sure do," Guy said. He glanced around to look at the women. They were three of the ugliest he'd ever seen. One was a pouting, obese slattern, another a worn-out crone, while the third was just a scowling, skinny whore. "I reckon I'll take the deer to the corral and start the butchering."

"Do it in the morning," Paulson said. "If you leave the meat around, the coyotes'll get it." He laughed. "And there ain't gonna be nobody in this bunch in condition to stand guard over it."

"I reckon not," Guy agreed. "I'll put her in the corner and tend to the chore tomorrow first chance." He carried the animal over to a far part of the house and set it down on the floor. It was then that he noticed Gustavo Fairweather sitting at a table drinking. Guy decided it was time to strike up a conversation with him. He walked over. "Howdy."

Fairweather looked up at him. "Howdy."

"I reckon that job went perty good," Guy said.

"Yeah," Fairweather said.

"When are you gonna bring us another'n?" Guy asked.

"I did tonight," Fairweather answered. "You was out hunting."

"Another stage?"

Fairweather shook his head. "You boys is gonna hit the Texas Central Railroad in a week. You're gonna have to leave by midday tomorrow."

"That's good," Guy said. "Where's this supposed to happen?"

"Between Longview and Marshall," Fairweather said. "Perty close to Louisiana."

"That's a long ride," Guy remarked.

"It'll be worth it," Fairweather assured him.

"What's the loot?"

"Gold pieces," Fairweather said. "Twenty-dollar ones. We got some just like 'em on another job a while back before you joined up with us."

"I always say you can't have enough gold coins," Guy said.

Fairweather flashed a rare smile. "Yeah."

The fat whore came over and sat down. She gave Guy her best seductive glance. It came across as a sort of drunken, heavy lidded stare. "I ain't seen you before."

"Nope. I'm new," Guy said.

"You're a cute feller," she said. "I like my men skinny."

"That's me," Guy said.

"You looking for a good time?" she asked.

"Lemme have a few drinks first, honey bunch," Guy said. "Then we'll see 'bout good times." He got to his feet and walked over to where several whiskey bottles were setting. He grabbed one and went off to the side of the room and sat down to watch the revelry. He pulled the cork and took a swallow.

It looked like he'd be able to get a note out to Charlie and Gideon this time. When the Texas Central Railroad got hit, there would be hell to pay and people dying.

Nine

The strikes of ax blades biting into the trees rang through the glen as Shorty Darnell, Willy Kemp, and Elmer Sherman labored at chopping down a few select specimens from a stand of cypress trees.

Six had already been felled and dragged by horses to lay across the railroad tracks that cut through the small forest where the site of the robbery had been chosen.

Ned Paulson, experienced at stopping trains for the purpose of looting them, was picky and argumentative when it came to placing the barriers just right.

"Do what I tell you dumb son of a bitches to do!" he shouted each time his outlaw charges became careless in their work. "If you're too far out, the engineer is gonna see 'em and come to a stop with plenty o' chance to back up. Remember your horses, which are a lot brighter'n any o' you, can't run as fast forward as a train can go backward!"

"We understand, Ned," Shorty assured him.

"On the other hand," Paulson continued. "If you put them trees too far ahead, the engineer'll come barreling straight across 'em at full speed and the whole damn train is gonna be derailed."

"What the hell's wrong with that?" Elmer Sherman wanted to know.

"On account o' all you got is a pile o' mashed cars all run together and you can't find shit in the mess, you dumb bastard! Ain't you ever seen how twisted up a train gets when it's derailed while running full out?" Paulson yelled. "Now put them things where I tell you to. It'll make the train stop, and we can jump aboard before he backs up."

The men obeyed his instructions to the letter as the logs were piled up to form the correct obstruction to stop the train. The whole job took three hours of hard toil, something men who chose to live on the owlhoot trail as outlaws did not like one bit.

When they finished, instead of having feelings of accomplishment, they complained:

"Damn! My arms is all tired out!" Elmer Sherman said. "It's gonna be hard to hold my shooting iron."

"Them logs is hard to roll around even with a horse to help," Shorty Darnell bellyached.

"I got blisters on my hands like a damn ditch-digger," Willy Kemp said. "They hurt!"

Paulson sneered. "You shoulda worn gloves like anybody with a lick o' sense would do."

Even Guy Tyrone was in a bad mood. "I hope we got time to rest up before we hold up that train. I'm too tuckered right now to worry about robbing some baggage car."

"All of you just shut up and listen," Paulson ordered them. "We ain't got time to stand around here crying like wored-out whores on a Saturday night. We got a goddamned train to rob. Now, I want Jess and Shorty on the far side o' the tracks. Keep an eye on anybody that might get off the train on that side and tries to sneak around to get a shot at us."

"We'll do it, Ned," Jess assured him.

Paulson continued his instructions. "Elmer and Lee, you two take the engineer. When the train stops, jump up in the cab with him and the fireman. Just throw down on 'em and make sure they don't try to take off. The best thing is have 'em stay away from the levers."

"You bet, Ned," Elmer said.

"Me, Guy, and Willy is gonna hit the baggage car," Ned said.

The thought made Guy nervous. He had managed to get a note out to the rock by the cottonwood telling Charlie Delano and Gideon Magee all the details of the planned train robbery. If they got the information, chances were good that when the baggage car door opened, there would be a swarm of hot lead flying out of it. Especially with someone like Gideon Magee, who always liked to shoot people instead of arresting them.

Ned noticed his obvious nervousness. "What's got a burr under your saddle, Guy?"

"It's all this damn work," Guy said with a weak grin. "I reckon I just ain't never got used to honest toil."

Paulson laughed. "Well, this time you're sweating for twenty-dollar gold pieces. That oughta make you feel better."

"Yeah," Guy said. "It oughta."

"Ever'body get into position," Paulson said. "And be ready to act quick."

The gang situated themselves as they had been ordered. Guy settled down on one side of the tracks with Paulson and Willy Kemp. He waved at Jess Garbel across from them.

"Don't forget not to let nobody sneak out on that side," Guy reminded him.

"You just get all them gold pieces," Jess replied. "I

don't want nothing left to roll around on the floor o' that baggage car."

"I'll get ever' one of 'em," Guy promised. He wasn't as sure as he sounded, since a picture of Gideon Magee greeting them in the door of the baggage car with blazing Colts flitted through his mind.

Paulson still noted Guy's nervousness. "Relax, will you, Guy? You're acting as skittish as a Texas jackrabbit trying to get past a rattlesnake in his hole."

"I never robbed a train before," Guy said. "I reckon that's why I'm on the nervous side."

"It's all set up," Paulson assured him. "We ain't got a thing to fret about."

"Are you sure?" Guy asked. Now he began to worry if Charlie Delano and Gideon Magee might be backshot by some crooked railroad guard while they faced the gang. That meant he would have to be looking out for his two friends.

"Ace Erickson knows what he's doing," Paulson said. "When he sets up a job, he does it right."

"Mmm," Guy mused. He had planned on hanging back to make sure he didn't get in the line of fire. But if he was going to have to cover Charlie and Gideon, he'd be moving up where the slugs would be flying. "Hell of a thing," he said aloud.

"What is?" Kemp asked.

"Uh, doing all that work o' chopping trees to get money the easy way," Guy answered, thinking fast.

"You're getting paid a hell of a lot better than any reg'lar woodcutter," Kemp said.

"I suppose," Guy said.

"You bet your ass you are," Paulson said. "You'll have twenty-dollar gold pieces jangling in your pockets afore you know it. A damn woodcutter wouldn't make that in half a year o' sweating his ass off."

Guy nodded. He reached around for a reassuring

touch of his jirara-wood billy club, then remembered that he had left the weapon behind when he took up the Ranger star. Too bad. It might have come in handy if a wild, swinging melee broke out. He turned his mind to other thoughts, studying the coolness of Ned Paulson.

The outlaw leader was smart, all right. He was a calm and sure hombre who knew exactly what he was doing. Guy figured he would try to keep a special eye on Ned Paulson when the shooting broke out.

A few moments of silence passed, then Elmer Sherman asked out loud what was on everybody's mind. "Can we go to Stavanger after this job?"

"We'll have to wait and see," Paulson said. "If we do good, I'm sure Ace is gonna give us a little extra reward."

"I tell you what I'd like to do," Lee Fenney said. "I'd like to put a bullet in that lawyer Banter's head."

"No you don't!" Paulson snapped. "Ace is the brains, but Banter handles getting all the information and arranging for pertection. Without him, we're goners.

"Yeah," Jess Garbel chimed in. "Why do you think we never get posses chasing after us at the ranch?"

"I still don't like the son of a bitch," Fenney insisted. "He thinks he's better'n anybody else."

"He's from back east," Paulson said. "What do you expect?"

"Train coming!" Shorty Darnell interrupted with a shout. "Listen!"

"I don't hear nothing," Willy Kemp said.

"Shut up and listen," Paulson said. "Shorty hears it."

"Shorty has the hearing of a jackrabbit," Jess Garbel said.

They strained their ears for a few more moments

before being rewarded with the distant sound of a locomotive.

"Let's get ready!" Paulson said. "It's time to go to work."

The men tensed, particularly Guy, who now had to cover his friends in the car—if they were there—and protect himself as well. He went from nervousness to outright agitation.

"This is some job," Guy said.

"Yeah," Paulson agreed.

The train came on. Then, when it appeared around the distant curve, the engineer sighted the logs piled on the tracks. He hit the brakes hard, knowing exactly what was going to happen. The man knew that only quick action would save his train from being robbed. The locomotive was still slowing down as its driver threw the engine into reverse. But it was too late. The big machine kept moving forward slower and slower as it wound down to a stop.

Up front, Elmer Sherman and Lee Fenney ran from their hiding places and scrambled up the steps into the cab. They threw down on the two men inside.

Sherman sneered, "Hands up, goddamn you! If one o' you so much as touches a lever, I'll blow his damn head off!"

Both trainmen, their faces pale with fear, raised their hands.

"Go sit down on the coal," Fenney said, motioning with his pistol.

They obeyed, settling down as best they could on the dirty lumps at the edge of the coal tender. When the pair realized they weren't going to be wantonly murdered, they relaxed some to wait out what they knew was a robbery.

Jess Garbel and Shorty Darnell watched the far side of the train from a hidden position in the brush up on the side of a hill bordering the tracks. They stood ready to shoot down anybody who dismounted from the cars.

At those precise moments, Guy, Ned Paulson, and Willy Kemp stormed the baggage car. Paulson yelled, "Open up in there or we'll dynamite you!"

A muffled voice inside called back, "Sure, mister. Gimme a chance to work the hasp."

"Hurry up!" Paulson commanded in a loud voice.

The door shook a bit, then slid open slowly at first. Suddenly it was jerked wide open.

A shotgun blast, windy and hot, rushed past Guy's face. He heard a whomping sound behind him and a gasp. Willy Kemp had caught the full force of the buckshot that hurled him off the railbed and down to the ground below.

Ned Paulson, snarling in fury, fired back at the car, his pistol barking with each squeeze of the trigger. Guy looked up and could see Gideon Magee swing up the barrel of a twelve-gauge sawed-off shotgun. It belched and flashed again as Paulson dove off the roadbed and fell beside Willy Kemp's mangled remains.

Guy and Gideon locked glances, then Captain Charlie Delano came into view for an instant before turning to the other side of the car. Guy now also jumped to cover, joining Paulson below. He rolled up next to him and saw what was left of Kemp.

"Oh, God!" Guy exclaimed.

"He won't be getting none o' the loot," Paulson casually observed between taking shots at the train.

"Can't hardly tell who he is," Guy said.

More firing came their way. Then others could be heard on the other side of the train.

"They're gonna get Jess and Shorty for sure. They ain't got a chance," Paulson said. "Let's get the hell out o' here." He jumped up and ran toward the horses with Guy following.

Now Sherman and Fenney could see what was happening. They quickly realized the train robbery had been stopped when they spotted Jess and Shorty sprawled on the ground where they'd fallen from behind the brush they had used as cover.

Sherman saw Guy and Paulson making a run for it. He shouted, "Let's clear out!"

They didn't even take time to shoot the engineer and fireman. The only thing on their minds was making a safe escape as they jumped down and took off after the other two.

Within a couple of minutes the robbery attempt was over and the four surviving members of the gang were riding like hell toward the west where the sanctuary of Denton County waited for them.

Fearful of a posse catching them before they were safe in their own territory, Paulson pressed on without regard to the horses. They skirted the town of Tatum, then swung back up between Kilgore and Tyler before he signaled them to slow down.

When they were finally able to talk, Elmer Sherman asked, "What the hell happened?"

"They was waiting for us," Paulson said. "Somebody tipped 'em off."

Guy kept silent, letting the others vent their anger and frustration. He was just glad he was still in one piece, not blown apart by either lawmen's or outlaws' guns.

"How could that be?" Fenney asked. "We're the ones that're supposed to have the inside information."

"Well, maybe ol' Maxwell Banter made a big mistake," Ned Paulson said. "I reckon this time his money didn't buy nothing but trouble for us."

"I told you I didn't like that lawyer son of a bitch!" Fenney said in anger.

"Jess and Shorty and Willy is dead," Sherman said.

"Are you sure about Jess and Shorty?" Paulson asked.

"Yeah," Sherman replied. "I seen 'em under fire and when they was hit. They fell outta them bushes like they was a coupla rag dolls."

"What're we gonna do now?" Guy asked nervously.

"We're gonna head back to the ranch," Paulson said. "Then I'm gonna go into Stavanger and have a talk with that damn lawyer."

"Can I go with you, Ned?" Fenney asked.

Paulson shook his head. "No. I'm gonna take Guy. He ain't been there before. It's about time he met Ace Erickson anyhow." He glanced around. "Boys, we ain't gonna be safe 'til we're back on that ranch. Let's ride for it!"

The quartet of failed train bandits jabbed spurs into their horses' sides and picked up speed to clear the hell out of eastern Texas.

Ten

Stavanger, Texas, was barely stirring in the early morning when Guy Tyrone and Ned Paulson, trail-dirty and travel-weary, rode up the main street on horses that were close to being blown. Both men showed the strain of not only the grueling trip they'd been on, but also from almost getting themselves blasted by the shotgun at the aborted train robbery.

Guy, his practiced eye developed as a sheriff in various towns, gave Stavanger a professional appraisal. He figured the place as a town that needed a cleaning up by professional starpackers. It was small, but the saloon called the Ace of Diamonds that dominated the main street was fancy and imposing. But even more telling than its appearance was the fact that it was the only drinking establishment in the place. That meant a town boss, and that was a sure sign of plenty of trouble for any decent folks living there. They would be the helpless and unfortunate innocents caught up in a situation like that.

"Here we are," Paulson said. "This is where the brains of our operation keep themselves."

"They don't seem too brainy to me after what happened to us," Guy said.

Paulson turned his horse in toward the hitching rack of the saloon. Guy followed him, also dismounting and flipping his reins over the rail. The two walked up to the saloon's door that was closed tight. Paulson banged on the portals.

A voice inside hollered, "We're closed."

"This is Paulson. I'm here to see Ace Erickson," he said testily. "Open the door. Now!"

"Just a minute," the voice said. After a bit of scuffling, the door opened and a bartender looked out at them. "Oh, hi, Ned. C'mon in. Mr. Erickson is back in his office." Not knowing Guy, he gave him a look of curiosity.

"Never mind," Guy said in a menacing tone. "You got more to worry about than me."

The bartender didn't want any trouble with the slim, young man. "Whatever you say."

"I hope Maxwell Banter is back there with the boss," Paulson said.

"He is," the bartender said quickly, returning to complete his pre-opening inventory of stock. "I think they're both anxious to see you."

"And I'm right anxious to see them," Paulson said, continuing to lead the way as they went to a door at the rear of the building. He rapped and called out, "Boss, it's me, Ned."

"Let yourself in, Ned," Ace Erickson called out.

Paulson opened the door. "Howdy."

Ace displayed a friendly smile. "How are you, Ned? Who is this with you?"

"This is a new man, name o' Guy Tyrone."

Guy nodded. "Howdy."

"That's Ace Erickson there," Paulson said. "And Mr. Banter."

"Welcome to the crew, Guy," Ace said with a

friendly nod. "I think Gustavo Fairweather mentioned meeting you. Have you settled in yet?"

"Not too good," Guy answered. "But I'll let Ned explain."

"Sounds serious," Ace replied. He glanced at Banter. "Doesn't it, Max?"

Maxwell Banter, sitting in a chair by the desk, gave Guy a disdainful look, then turned his attention back to his cup of coffee.

Ace smiled. "You didn't waste any time getting here after the job. Are the boys that anxious for their cuts?"

"There ain't no cuts, Boss," Paulson said. "As soon as that goddamned baggage door opened, hot lead instead o' cold gold poured out at us."

Now Maxwell Banter was interested. He got to his feet. "What?" he asked anxiously.

Paulson glared at the lawyer. "That's right. The first thing that come at us was a shotgun blast." He pointed to Guy. "It damn near took his head off."

"Willy Kemp was right behind me. He got it full in the chest," Guy said.

"Jess and Shorty died o' lead poisoning too," Paulson said. "I don't know if it was the law or railroad detectives in that car, but they was squatting in there waiting for us." He kept an angry eye on Maxwell Banter. "We was bushwhacked."

Ace frowned in puzzlement at Banter. "I thought that was all set up."

"It was, Ace," Banter said. "I can't figure out what could have gone wrong. My contact said no one suspected anything. There was only going to be a couple of men in the baggage car."

"There was four or five," Paulson said.

Guy thought it best to keep things as confused as

possible by garbling the facts. He didn't want any good information getting back to anyone who might figure out what happened. "I think there was more, Ned. I swear I seen a dozen. I think they was railroad detectives."

"They couldn't be!" Banter exclaimed. "My contact is one of the detectives for that line. He assured me that only a couple of clerks would be there. One would be our man who would pop the door open the minute the robbery started."

Guy made a mental note to mention a railroad detective and baggage-car clerk as part of Erickson's gang. Charlie Delano could do something with that.

Erickson walked to the door and hollered out at the bartender. "Go fetch Gustavo Fairweather quick." He closed the door. "We've got to get some more men."

"We sure as hell do, Boss," Paulson agreed. "All that's left is me, Guy, Lee Fenney, and Elmer Sherman. That ain't enough to pull off any jobs even if they're fixed in advance." He looked at Banter. "And if things ain't fixed proper, we'll all be wiped out on the next one anyhow."

"You listen to me, Paulson!" Banter snapped at him. "This is the first one that went wrong. So don't start getting high-handed with me."

"If your sneaky friends don't foller through, I'm likely to get killed," Paulson said in a low, cold tone. "So I'm gonna get real high-handed."

Ace Erickson spoke up. "We'll not get anywhere by becoming angry with each other. Something went wrong this time. We've paid a price. What we must do is find out what it was, and make sure it doesn't happen again."

Guy didn't want them to find out a thing. He decided to stir things up some more. "It's hard enough to rob a train under normal circumstances. And it's a hell of a situation when you're expected and they're ready and waiting for you."

"You shut up!" Banter snarled.

Guy scowled. Here was a chance to throw some blame around. "If you can't fix things up, at least don't warn 'em about us." He decided to elaborate a bit more with some exaggeration. "Jess Garbel was an old friend o' mine. We was in prison together."

"I told you to shut up!" Banter yelled.

"Everybody shut up!" Ace Erickson commanded. "I don't want any arguments or accusations. This won't solve anything. We're in a dangerous business and things can go wrong now and then."

A knock on the door was quickly followed by Sheriff Gustavo Fairweather's entrance into the office. "Joe said you wanted to see me, Ace."

"Yeah," Erickson said. "We've lost three men on this last job."

"Yeah," Paulson said. "Shorty, Jess, and Willy."

"What happened?" Fairweather asked.

"They was waiting for us, Gustavo," Paulson said. "The damn baggage car door opened and there was twelve or so railroad detectives in there shooting like the Fourth o' July."

"I think maybe they was fifteen of 'em," Guy said.

Fairweather sighed. "That's bad. I rcckon you boys are shorthanded now."

"We ain't got enough to do things proper," Paulson said.

"Looks like I'm gonna have to do some hiring," Fairweather said.

"Right," Ace said. "We've got to have more than

four men. And we want some damned good ones."

"That's the only kind I know, Ace," Fairweather said confidently.

Erickson pointed to Maxwell Banter "In the meantime, I want you to find out what went wrong. If things just got out of your contact's control, that's one thing. If he's pulled a double cross, then—"

"—then I'll deal with it," Fairweather said. "That's something we can't let slide."

"I'll leave for Dallas today," Banter said.

"What do you want us to do, Boss?" Paulson asked.

"You boys lay low out at the ranch," Erickson said. "Tell everybody that we'll find out what went wrong. In the meantime, I'll send out some women and whiskey. That should put them back into a better mood." He thought a moment. "And I'll give 'em each a quick hundred in greenbacks to make up for losing out on a good cut."

"The boys will appreciate that, Boss," Paulson said.

"Makes me feel better," Guy said agreeably. He had to admit that Erickson treated his men right. The outlaw boss knew how to buy loyalty.

Ace went over to his safe in the corner of the room. After working the combination, he took out four hundred dollars. He tossed the bundles to Paulson. "Tell the boys the women and whiskey should be there by day after tomorrow. And you two treat yourselves to some drinks before you head out."

"Thanks, Boss. We'll go back after we wet our whistles," Paulson said. "Both of us and our horses is damn near done in."

"Nice meeting you, Boss," Guy said, following Paulson out to the saloon. They went to the bar and bellied up.

Paulson signaled to the barkeep. "The boss says to give us a snort or two."

"You bet, Ned," the man said. He set up a bottle with a couple of glasses.

Guy quickly poured himself a stiff drink and tossed it down. "That was a real dust-cutter."

A feminine voice interrupted the drinking. "How'd it go, Ned?"

Guy, startled, turned and looked into the face of the most beautiful woman he had ever seen. He grinned. "Howdy, ma'am.

"Hello," she said, looking intently into Guy's handsome face. "I don't think I've seen you before."

Paulson introduced them. "Miss Dinah, this is our new man Guy Tyrone."

Guy nodded to her. He could tell she found him pleasing. That was something he always enjoyed with women. "I'm pleased to meet you, Miss Dinah."

"And I'm pleased to meet you," she said. "Mind if I join you two for a drink?"

Paulson also sensed the woman's attraction to Guy. He spoke quickly. "We got to go."

"Ace said we could have a couple of snorts," Guy protested.

"And I say we're going," Paulson said. "Good-bye, Miss Dinah."

Guy smiled at her. "I'll see you again. I'm sure."

"I hope so," she said.

"Let's go, Guy!" Paulson snapped.

They went outside to their horses. Guy was testy about leaving so quickly. "How come we couldn't stay there and talk to that pretty gal?"

"I'm saving your damn life," Paulson said. "That's Ace Erickson's woman and he don't want nobody getting extra friendly toward her."

"That's a shame," Guy said. The two mounted up and headed out of town for Grogan's ranch. "That was right nice of Ace Erickson giving us each a hundred dollars like that."

"Yeah," Paulson said in agreement. "He figures it as an investment. A little extra touch buys loyalty."

"Don't it, though," Guy remarked.

The pair rode slowly across the countryside, keeping to cover as much as possible. They feared no posse or lawmen would be out hunting them in Denton County. But it was always best in that line of work to keep out of sight as much as possible. They went down into draws, followed creeks, and rode through stands of trees. Only when the terrain was too rough for travel did they get on the open trails. By the time they got back to the ranch, it was late afternoon.

"I think I'll try to get another deer or a coupla rabbits," Guy said. "The thought of more biscuits and beans turns my stomach."

"The boys will appreciate that," Paulson said. He reached back and pulled a pack of bills from his saddlebags. He tossed it over. "You might as well get your cut now."

"Thanks, Ned," Guy said.

"I want to warn you again about Miss Dinah," Paulson said. "She's poison as far as you're concerned. Savvy?"

"Sure," Guy said with an easy grin. "I ain't given her another thought. It's hunting time, so I'll see you later. Wish me luck."

"I sure as hell do," Paulson said with a grin and wink. "I'm hungry too."

Guy rode out of the ranch yard with a feeling of regret beginning to build up in his gut. He had begun to tire of his role as a spy. Somehow he felt like a backshooter after Jess Garbel, a man he'd known before, along with two others died when the job between Longview and Marshall went awry. Guy knew he would have to have a long, hard talk with Captain Charlie Delano about the situation. Sneaking around behind other men's backs wasn't his style.

Guy rode past the cottonwood tree where he was supposed to leave messages, heading straight for the camp where Charlie and Gideon should be. He only stopped a couple of times to make sure no one was following from the ranch. When he was thoroughly convinced he was all by himself, he went straight to the bivouac and found the other two Texas Rangers.

Guy dismounted and hobbled his horse in front of their cookfire. "I hope you two son of a bitches is happy," he said. "I almost got my head blowed off by a shotgun poking outta that train."

"That was me," Gideon said.

"I *know* it was you!" Guy snapped. "I seen you."

Gideon went on. "I shot the feller behind you."

"That don't make me feel much better," Guy said. He squatted down and helped himself to the coffee. "I'm tuckered, let me tell you."

"We ain't exactly fresh ourselves," Charlie said. "We left the train in Longview and come straight back here. We got back early this morning."

"Well, I come by way of Stavanger," Guy said. "And I finally met Ace Erickson." He glanced at Charlie. "I think your plan has gone to hell. Shooting up three men ain't doing nothing to that gang.

Ol' Gustavo Fairweather is hiring some new pistoleros as quick as he can. So, Erickson still can't be reached."

Gideon wasn't worried. "Next time we'll have to kill ever' one o' the bastards."

"Yeah?" Guy said. "Just remember I ain't a real member of that gang when you start massacring 'em."

"Sure," Gideon said with a slow smile. "I'll work on that, Guy."

"We're gonna have to get a setup where we can get 'em all in one fell swoop, that's for sure," Charlie said. "And as quick as that's did, we'll move into Stavanger and take out Erickson and Gustavo Fairweather."

"At any rate, I got some news for you," Guy said. "The inside men on that job for Erickson was one o' the railroad's detectives and a baggage-car clerk."

"What're their names?" Charlie asked.

"Don't you think I'd tell you if I knowed?" Guy asked. "I just can't figger out how you two got on that car."

"It was easy," Charlie said. "We used the authority granted us by the Texas Rangers and just rode along. As soon as the train stopped for the robbery, we went into action."

"You was lucky you wasn't backshot by somebody," Guy pointed out. "I think one o' them fellers was on the train."

"We kept on the alert," Gideon said.

"I did too," Guy said. "Hell! I had to!"

"You knowed this job was dangerous," Charlie pointed out.

"I ain't bellyaching about that," Guy said. "But let me tell you something. I feel like a backshooter doing all this spying. I'm getting to know them fellers. I ain't exactly pals with 'em, but when you ride with other men a feeling develops between you. A loyalty, if you know what I mean."

"Now let *me* tell *you* something," Charlie said. "Them new pals o' yours is killers. They'll murder innocent bank tellers or baggage-car clerks to get their way. The son of a bitches is a blight on the great state o' Texas. And if you're a true Texan, you'll do whatever it takes to get rid of 'em."

"They're lower'n snakes' bellies, Guy," Gideon said. "They don't deserve no consideration or fair play 'cause they sure as hell ain't gonna live by any kind o' rules themselves."

"Getting rid o' them bastards is gonna save innocent lives," Charlie added.

Guy was thoughtful for several moments. "It don't seem so bad when you put it in that light."

"You got to keep your eyes and ears open," Charlie said. "As soon as you can get the news of another job, write up ever'thing you know and put it under that rock by the cottonwood. We're gonna be working on getting ever' one of 'em the first chance we get."

"Like I said, fellers," Guy cautioned him. "Keep in mind I'll be in the middle of the crowd."

"You'll have to figger out when to pull back," Charlie said. "We can't help you none on that."

"Sure," Guy said. "I can take care of myself. At least I better." He finished the coffee and stood up. "Well, I gotta go get rabbit or a deer or something."

"Good luck," Charlie said.

"That's a real dumb thing to say to a feller in my situation," Guy said. "If I had any good luck I wouldn't be where I am today."

"At least you're making extry money," Gideon pointed out. "Except for this last job maybe."

Guy grinned to himself. He'd decided not to tell them about the hundred dollars.

Eleven

Guy Tyrone came awake slowly, almost hesitantly, as if even in sleep he subconsciously knew that a great deal of discomfort awaited him when he entered the world of full wakefulness. The final act of regaining full consciousness brought unwelcome and painful sensations to the Ranger as his head pounded with an awful ache.

Guy licked his lips and noted that his mouth seemed as dry as the sands of southwestern Texas. He started to sit up, but the movement caused an increase to the pain in his skull, so he slowly lay back down.

"I musta been mule-kicked!" he whispered in agony. "Mule-kicked and dragged by the heels through a cactus patch. That's the only thing that can explain this much hurting."

Once more, this time very deliberately and carefully, he raised himself. His stomach churned so much that for a couple of moments he thought he would be throwing up everything he'd ever eaten before in his entire life. But slowly his belly settled down to an angry murmur.

Taking a deep breath, Guy was finally sitting up and able to look around to see where the hell he was. He lay on a narrow plank bench near a wall in Grogan's ranch house. After as much as he drank the previous night, he wouldn't have been surprised no matter where he was.

After taking a second, more detailed look at his surroundings, Guy spoke again in a hoarse voice to himself. "A tornado must've hit us."

The scene his bleary eyes beheld was that of the shabby ranch house with three sleeping men and two slumbering women scattered throughout overturned furniture, broken bottles, and other debris that littered the rustic building. Smoke from a dying fire in the fireplace drifted across the chamber adding a near macabre aspect to what he saw.

Slowly Guy began to recall what had transpired the previous evening.

The wagon with two women from Stavanger arrived about an hour after he returned to the ranch from visiting with Charlie Delano and Gideon Magee. The females had a barrel of whiskey and a keg of beer with them. These were extra presents from Ace Erickson to soothe the ruffled feelings of his men. And the ploy worked. Ned Paulson, Lee Fenney, and Elmer Sherman quickly forgot the deaths of their friends at the botched train robbery as they fetched the liquor and females inside for a night of unceasing revelry.

The two women hadn't been among the ugly ones sent out before. These two were rather decent looking. It seemed Ace Erickson sincerely wanted to make up to the boys for almost getting them killed at the train.

"Ain't it thoughtful of the boss to feel sorry for us?" Lee Fenney remarked.

"Yeah," Elmer Sherman agreed. "This is gonna be a real nice evening."

But there wasn't much niceness as time went on. The basis of the trouble was the fact that these particular women were truly good-looking.

Fenney and Sherman both immediately took a fancy to the same one. Rather than take turns with the dancehall girl, each wanted her as their own for the entire evening. A fistfight broke out between them that Ned Paulson quickly broke up.

The incident took the spirit of fun out of the party, and everyone settled down to some deep, quick drinking out of the two barrels. The women, a bit frightened at being isolated with the gang after the trouble started, turned out not to be pleasant company. They stuck to themselves as Fenney and Sherman glared at each other, getting drunker and drunker. Eventually they got into another fight that Paulson, because he was so intoxicated, could barely get under control.

As the evening drifted by, the women also became drunk and lost their nervousness. That was the cause of the real trouble. They allowed themselves to be drawn into the conflict, and a shrieking contest broke out between them as they took sides.

Guy, bored and feeling low, simply watched the goings-on while sipping whiskey from a tin cup. He kept to himself at one of the tables, avoiding any participation in the ruckus. After several hours, he was pretty drunk himself, but he still managed to keep his temper and behavior under control.

Sometime, during the wee hours of the morning following a period of quiet, a minor riot broke out as the others, thoroughly intoxicated, angry, and rowdy, went after each other in a free-for-all. Guy watched it all through his own personal whiskey haze, noting crashing furniture, falling bodies, cussing, yelling, punching, and kicking until things slowly eased down until one last person was standing. That was Ned Paulson. But the outlaw leader only lasted a minute or two more. Finally, weaving and staggering, he finally crashed facedown on the floor where he still lay amongst the debris.

Then Guy passed out.

Now, the party finished and his hangover settled in fierce and relentless, Guy got to his feet and lurched across the room to the door. He stepped outside and took a deep breath of fresh air. It cleared his head a little and got rid of some of the ache. Dawn had just peaked and the sun was on its way toward its proper place in the midmorning sky. The heat of the day was a couple of hours away, so it was cool and refreshing. Guy felt another minor rumble in his stomach, but that feeling of sickness also evaporated.

At that moment he wished the whole episode with Ace Erickson and the gang was done with. He wanted to be out of the Texas Rangers and get back to the simple life of being a town sheriff like he'd been in Sweetwater.

Whenever Guy Tyrone felt low or out of sorts, he preferred to be alone. He knew that the only way he would be able to enjoy solitude when the others woke up was to be away on a horseback ride. On the way to the corral to get his horse, he stopped at the well long enough to get a drink of the cool water.

"Damn!" he said to himself after swishing the liquid around in his mouth. "I swear a little dawg must've shit on my tongue last night."

He went over to the corral and leaned against it, feeling tired and sick. After a couple of minutes of deep breathing, Guy forced himself to go through the gate and pull his saddle off the top rail.

The Ranger staggered under the weight of the heavy device as he approached his horse. An attempt to throw it on the animal's back ended with the saddle going over the horse and landing on the ground.

"I don't think things is gonna go my way today," Guy said.

The horse looked quizzically at him, then pulled away as it sensed something different about its owner.

"Now looky, horse. I'm hungover and feel like I been run down by a twenty-mule-team wagon going at the gallop," he said. "This here saddle is going up on your back or I'm gonna shoot you." He stared bleary-eyed at his horse. "Are you ready? Here we go."

The next time, he managed to get the saddle up on the horse's back, but the stallion moved away, sending it falling to the dirt once more. Guy pulled his pistol and pointed it at the animal.

"I told you, you lop-eared son of a bitch, that I'm gonna shoot you if you don't let me put this saddle on your back," he said. "Now! Goddamn it! Stand still!"

The horse sensed the man's anger and instinctively did as it knew it should. The saddle went on and was cinched up. Guy stared at his handiwork. "Oh, damn! I forgot the blanket."

Off came the saddle, on went the blanket, and on went the saddle again. Guy cinched it up. "At least your bridle's on," he said. "I don't have to worry about that." Guy led the horse out of the fenced-in area and closed the gate. Then he took a deep breath. "Now I got to get on, don't I?"

He stuck his foot in the stirrup and lost his balance, falling onto his back. He rolled over on his hands and knees and got up again.

"Nope. Things sure ain't gonna go my way."

A couple of more attempts had to be made before he was able to pull himself up into a proper seat. Guy wasn't sure where he wanted to go. It didn't matter, as long as he got away to be by himself until he felt better. He flicked the reins and let the horse have its head. The mount walked slowly from the corral and crossed the ranch yard, heading for open country.

A sound in the distance attracted Guy's attention. He looked in the direction it came from for a few minutes before seeing Gustavo Fairweather leading a dozen other horsemen toward the ranch. Guy reined in and waited.

Fairweather led the others up to him and signaled the group to come to a halt. Stavanger's sheriff looked closely at Guy. "What the hell's the matter with you?"

"Too much whiskey last night," Guy said. "Does it show?"

"It sure as hell does," Fairweather said. "I seen

corpses that got better color than you."

"Corpses is luckier'n me," Guy said. "They can't feel nothing."

Fairweather snorted. "Where's the boys?"

"The rest o' the fellers and them gals is in the house fast asleep," Guy answered.

Fairweather laughed. "Asleep or passed out?"

"Take your choice," Guy said.

"And where the hell are you going?" Fairweather asked.

"For a ride to clear my head," Guy said.

"Well, you can turn around," Fairweather told him. "We got business to discuss. I want ever'body to be there."

"Are you loco?" Guy asked. "You ain't gonna get nothing out o' them others. I told you, they're in there unconscious."

"Then we'll wake 'em all up," Fairweather said. "Now turn around."

Wordlessly, Guy pulled on the reins of his horse and rode back to the house with the group of men following. When he reached the front door, he dismounted. Without waiting, he pushed open the door and went inside. Gustavo Fairweather and the others got off their horses and followed him into the interior.

The scene inside hadn't changed one bit. None of the sleeping people had even rolled into different positions, much less awakened from their night of celebration and fighting.

Guy gestured at the mess. "What'd I tell you?"

"God!" Fairweather exclaimed. "Ain't this a sight?" He took a deep breath and yelled, "Ever'body wake up! C'mon, goddamn it! Let's go!

Wake up!" He waded into the scene, giving Ned Paulson, Lee Fenney, and Elmer Sherman vicious kicks that rolled them over.

Paulson was the first to reenter the world of the living. He rubbed his side where he'd been kicked and sat up. "What the hell's going on?" he asked in a moaning voice.

"You sleeping beauties wake up," Fairweather said. "And the whores too."

Paulson looked up at the sheriff. "Where the hell did you come from?"

"Stavanger, where else?" Fairweather answered. "And I brought your new gang with me."

Paulson looked around at the newcomers. "Them fellers?"

"Who else?" Fairweather remarked.

By then all the men had crowded into the smelly, dank interior. They grinned at the sight, nudging each other as they looked at the females.

"Don't get no ideas," Fairweather warned them. "Them women is going to leave now." He walked over to one and grabbed her by the arm. Dragging her over to the other, he got the second woman in the same manner and went toward the door with his living load that began to come awake.

"Ow!" one exclaimed. Her eyes opened and she tried to comprehend what was going on. "Lemme go! Lemme go!"

Fairweather took them through the door and dropped them on the dirt. "Get your money-making asses up on that wagon and head back for Stavanger. Now!" he barked.

Both women, wide-awake enough to realize it was Gustavo Fairweather giving them orders, kept their mouths shut as they got to their feet. Numb, dizzy, and still sleepy, the pair staggered toward the vehicle.

Fairweather sent a couple of the new men to hitch up the team to the conveyance, then went inside to make sure that Ned Paulson, Lee Fenney, and Elmer Sherman were up and moving.

Guy went over to one of the tables and sat down, his head in his hands as the ache pounded through his skull once more. "Can't this wait?" he moaned.

Paulson sat down beside him. "You got a job for us, Gustavo?"

"What the hell do you think brings me out to this neck of the woods? Your charming company?" Fairweather said. "There's a bank in Waco that needs your attention."

The rest of the new men were all inside now. They crowded around the wall and waited to see what was going to happen. But before Gustavo Fairweather could say anything, one of them stepped forward and looked at Guy.

"I know you," he said.

Guy, bleary-eyed, looked up. The man seemed vaguely familiar. "Do I owe you any money?"

"No," the man said.

"Then don't worry about it none," Guy advised him.

"But I owe *you* something—an ass-kicking," the outlaw said.

"There's so many son of a bitches that want to kick my butt that you'll have to stand in line," Guy said.

"This feller was a deputy sheriff in Sweetwater,"

the man said aloud. "He's a goddamned star-packer."

Ned Paulson sneered. "Hell, we know that. Guy Tyrone's been on both sides o' the law."

"Yeah? Well, he's a Texas Ranger, goddamn it!" the man said. "I know, 'cause I seen him swore into the Rangers right in front o' my eyes after he throwed me in jail."

Guy quickly looked up. Now he recognized the man as Ed Hall, whom he'd disarmed in the Sweetwater saloon. Guy remembered that Captain Charlie Delano had talked him into joining the Rangers while Hall listened in his cell.

Fairweather frowned. "You been swore into the Texas Rangers, Tyrone?"

"Aw, hell," Guy said. "That feller is loco. If I was a Texas Ranger, what the hell would I be doing here?"

Gustavo looked closely at him. "Maybe you're working against us, Tyrone."

Guy sensed the situation was about to erupt into serious trouble for him. He could keep calm and hope for the best, or figure straight off that the situation would go to hell.

Guy made a quick decision.

He came up with his leather cleared and the Colt in his hand. "The first son of a bitch that bats an eye gets a slug." He motioned them all away from the door. "I'll take two or three before you get me," Guy warned them. "I got nothing to lose."

"Don't move," Fairweather told his men. "Let this son-of-a-bitching Ranger do what he thinks he's got to do."

Guy moved toward the door glad that his horse was outside and saddled up. He backed through the flimsy portal, then slammed it shut. After two quick shots at the cabin he raced for his horse and leaped into the saddle, his hangover forgotten.

Guy kicked his mount into a wild gallop as he left the ranch in a rush. As he continued his dash for safety he could hear the shouts of the gang emerging from the house. Seconds later, shots split the air around him.

He gritted his teeth and whispered to himself, "Things truly just ain't going my way today!"

Twelve

The quick physical exertion of making an escape after momentarily forgetting the effect of the previous night's drinking quickly caught up with Guy Tyrone as he bounced around in the saddle during the wild ride from Grogan's ranch.

His disposition didn't improve a bit when he noted that the gang had wasted no time in mounting a hot pursuit after him.

Guy's vision blurred and the pain in his head went from a throbbing ache to a constant pain that made a loud buzzing in his ears. Only the reports of shots behind him broke through the droning sound.

Those bullets also kept him concentrating on the job at hand of getting the hell out of there in one piece.

Guy headed for a dry creekbed he'd found while out hunting. There were some tall trees bordering the gash in the earth that would provide him with some protective covering as he tried to put distance between himself and his pursuers.

He kicked the horse's flanks to hurry the animal along. After reaching his destination, Guy bounded down the narrow confines for a hundred yards. When he reached a good place to head to higher ground, he veered upward out of the creekbed. A quick gallop across an open space led to woods. Rather than enter the trees, he made another turn to skirt them.

From there Guy was in open country, and the only option open there was speed. That was where he could really shine. His stallion was fast.

"Ha-yah!" Guy yelled. "Go, horse!"

The animal, instinctively picking up both the excitement of the chase and the smell of fear in its rider, kicked loose into a wide-open run without holding back any effort. Its hooves crashed down on the Texas terrain in a rapid staccato of clod-kicking pounding.

Guy wanted to get help from Charlie Delano and Gideon Magee as quickly as possible, but he had to do it in a way that they wouldn't have their hiding place betrayed to the outlaw gang. If he wasn't careful, his two friends would be overrun and shot down like trapped rabbits. The best way to pull it off, he figured, was to bring the chase as close to their camp as possible so they would hear the noise and investigate. Both were experienced gunmen who could come up with a proper reaction. With their help, the pursuit could be broken up or at least delayed long enough so he could make a getaway.

The idea should work beautifully, provided Charlie and Gideon hadn't gone off to Dallas for the day.

Hoping for the best, Guy moved in the direction of their camp. He planned to head straight for the location, then make a quick flanking movement to the south. If nothing else, he could hope to run all the way to Dallas and get the hell out of Denton County. A glance back showed that his persistent pursuers would never allow that. They were already spreading out to cut off any more maneuvering on his part. The angle of their pursuit made it obvious that it was only a matter of time before they caught up with him. Guy's safety depended entirely on Charlie Delano and Gideon Magee.

Guy headed straight for the copse of trees that hid his two partners' camp. When he drew in close, he made a wild pull on the reins and rode in a southerly direction.

"Hey!" he yelled in the desperate hope of alerting them. "Hey! Hey!"

He glanced back at the gang and noted they were no longer shooting at him. But that wasn't good news. That simply meant they were now concentrating on getting in closer for the kill.

"C'mon, horse!" Guy yelled. "Ha-yah!"

The chase headed back into open country. Guy wanted to try another run toward the location where Charlie and Gideon's camp was located, but the maneuvering of the outlaws had effectively cut him off. A few more hopeful, quick glances back also told him that his fellow Rangers weren't in their camp. Guy damned them to hell for being in Dallas having a good time while he had Ace Erickson's gang hot on his heels.

He spotted a long gully common in that part of the country a few hundred yards away and headed for it. It was deep enough to keep him out of sight for a bit, which meant if he could get inside, he would be hidden momentarily and the gang wouldn't be able to figure out which direction he would be taking. A little hesitation on their part could buy him some precious distance.

Riding full-tilt and hell-for-leather, Guy charged into the thick vegetation. The ground there was more uneven than he had anticipated, and the horse stumbled a bit and bucked in instinctive fear of injury.

"Easy, damn it!" Guy pleaded. But the stallion didn't like the hemmed-in area where he couldn't see. In protest, the horse bucked nervously as Guy fought to stay in the saddle.

He lost.

Almost before he was aware of it, Guy tumbled out of the saddle, hitting the ground and rolling uncontrollably almost a dozen times before coming to a stop. Now, disoriented and bruised, he pulled his pistol from its holster and turned to face his pursuers. The tumbling fall he'd endured had resulted in extreme dizziness. Unable to keep his balance, Guy fell to the ground, trying to focus his blurred vision. Through the haze of confusion and fear he realized this would be his last stand.

Shots blasted out nearby.

Guy winced and shuddered as he waited for the heavy slugs to crash into his body. Several more quick seconds of shooting followed before he realized the firing was going in a direction *out* of the gully rather than coming into it. He struggled up to a kneeling position, now able to see clearly. Guy caught the sight of Gideon Magee in the bushes making well-aimed deliberate shots with his Winchester.

"Hey!" Guy called out.

"Hey, yourself," Gideon answered without letting up on his shooting.

"Where's Charlie?"

"Yonder," Gideon answered with a flick of his head toward the end of the gully.

Guy looked in the direction indicated and could see Charlie Delano behind a tree. He, too, was using a carbine as he sent well-spaced, accurate shots into the gang.

A few weak, sporadic fusillades splattered in the Rangers' direction, then died out. The outlaws pulled back to better cover. After a couple of minutes they galloped away.

Gideon laughed. "They think you've drawed 'em into a trap."

Charlie Delano walked over and looked at Guy. "Are you all right?"

"I reckon," Guy said. With the dizziness now gone, he got to his feet and looked around for his horse. Guy spotted where the stallion had come to a stop in the trees. The animal, calmed down, had begun to graze on the sweet grass around the brush.

Gideon joined the pair. "Them son of a bitches is gone."

"You wouldn't mind telling us how you got them pals o' yours so riled at you, would you?" Charlie asked. "You ain't been cheating at cards, have you?"

"I don't like to play cards," Guy said angrily.

"Then what got 'em wise to you?" Charlie insisted on knowing.

"Do you remember that jasper I had the fight

with in the jailhouse in Sweetwater?" Guy asked.

"The one you whupped on with the billy club o' yours? Sure, a little, I reckon," Charlie said.

"Well, the son of a bitch showed up right in the middle o' the new men that Gustavo Fairweather brung in to replace the ones killed at the train robbery," Guy said.

"Attempted train robbery," Gideon pointed out. *"Attempted!* Me and Charlie broke it up, remember?"

"Yeah. I remember that and a load o' hot buckshot flying past my head," Guy said. "Anyhow, this feller remembered me getting swore into the Texas Rangers."

Gideon chuckled. "Didn't that set well with Gustavo Fairweather?"

"Let me say that all of a sudden I felt like a drunk in church," Guy said. "Nobody really wanted me around."

"They wanted to see you dead from the looks o' things," Charlie said. "How many new men do they have?"

"They got twelve more," Guy answered. "Add that to the three there and—" He counted on his fingers. "—fifteen of 'em. That's how many there is now in that gang. That's a lot o' fellers to have chase you."

"How'd you know where we was?" Gideon asked.

"I didn't," Guy said. "I was hoping to lead 'em close to your camp, then veer away so's you two could give me a hand."

"Well, we wasn't there," Charlie said.

"So I noticed," Guy complained. "I figgered you

two had gone into Dallas and was drinking cold beer and dancing with pretty gals."

"Naw," Gideon said. "We just moved the camp."

"We didn't want to get found out if you was discovered and whipped into telling about us and where we was camped out," Charlie said.

"How in hell did you expect me to find you, then?" Guy asked irritably. "If I wanted to talk to you or give you some information, I could've rode around here for days or weeks and never figgered out where you was."

"That's why we had the rock by the cottonwood," Charlie explained. "You could've left us notes there."

"Piss on that cottonwood!" Guy snapped.

"Only if you're a dawg," Gideon said with a guffaw.

"You're really funny, Gideon," Guy sneered. "A real caution. That's you."

"We ain't got time for more talking," Charlie pointed out. "Them outlaws is gonna regroup and come back here to find us."

"Well, I'm as packed and ready to go as I can be," Guy said. "I had to leave most o' my gear back at that hideout." He went over and got his horse by the reins, bringing it back with him. "I'll be borrowing some blankets from you later. But right now I'd suggest you two break camp."

"We ain't got much choice," Charlie said. "Especially since you've invited the most notorious outlaw gang in Texas to come calling."

"I thought you'd be thrilled to meet 'em," Guy said sardonically.

"Which direction we headed, Charlie?" Gideon asked as he began to gather up his gear.

"South," Charlie said. "Toward Dallas."

"I got a better idea," Guy said. "Let's go through Dallas and keep moving south."

"That'd take us too far away from Ace Erickson," Charlie pointed out. "I don't care if he's got fifteen or a hundred and fifteen men in that gang, we're gonna get 'em. So we won't be heading south."

"But it would take us to Waco," Guy said.

"Waco?" Gideon asked. "You want to go hide in Waco?"

"No," Guy answered. "I want to go there to break up a bank robbery."

Charlie stopped what he was doing and looked at his younger friend. "Are you saying Erickson's gang is going to hit a bank in Waco?"

"That's exactly what I'm saying," Guy replied smugly.

"Which bank is it?"

"I don't know," Guy said.

"When is the job supposed to be pulled?" Gideon wanted to know.

"I don't know," Guy said.

"That ain't a hell of a lot to go on," Gideon complained. "You're damn near saying that we just can't get there from here."

"I'll tell you something, though," Charlie interjected. "If Gustavo Fairweather brought in a new gang and has a job for 'em, it's gonna be a mighty big one."

"Did Fairweather say he had a job in Waco?" Gideon asked.

"Sure. He was talking about it when he first got there, but when that feller Ed Hall remembered seeing me become a Ranger, Gustavo got side-tracked," Guy said.

"And I'll bet he forgot he mentioned anything about the job while Guy was around," Charlie said.

"So what're we gonna do? Go down to Waco and wait around 'til we see 'em?" Gideon asked.

"You got any other ideas?" Charlie asked.

Gideon shook his head. "Nope. Let's get packed up and on the trail."

Charlie and Gideon set about breaking up the camp. They deftly rolled up their blankets, packed away cooking gear, and took the extra clothing hung up on nearby tree branches for airing out, shoving the duds into saddlebags. After saddling and bridling their horses, the two lawmen were ready to go.

Guy swung himself up into the saddle. "About time," he said testily. "C'mon, boys."

"Lead the way," Charlie said. "If you're in such an all-fire hurry."

The trio of starpackers rode out of the trees, turning south across the prairie toward Dallas. They rode easily, traversing the flat landscape at a regular pace while keeping a sharp eye out for any potential bushwhackers. None would have been surprised if Gustavo Fairweather decided to try a sneaky ride-around to get ahead of them and lay a trap. Any ambush site was carefully avoided, even if it meant going out of their way.

They reached Dallas when the sun was high overhead. They skirted the city to keep from being delayed by its crowded streets. Traveling in silent determination, the three Rangers cut back in a southeastern direction, making their way around the city. The ride took them through Mexican *barrios* that were wide open with small plots of land between the clusters of adobe houses.

Then it was back into the open countryside again, but this time following the well-traveled dirt road that led them along the seventy-nine-mile journey to Waco. It was easy traveling with plenty of company. Stagecoaches, wagons, individual riders, and buggies followed the well-kept dirt highway either heading north or south toward their individual destinations.

Charlie, Guy, and Gideon kept going until deciding to make camp at dusk. The trio settled beside the roadway to cook a hurried meal, then relax a bit before turning in. Several weary travelers spotted them and accepted the customary invitations to spend the night around their campfire that was part of trail etiquette.

It was a friendly atmosphere with the other road-weary men. A couple of bottles were pulled from saddlebags and passed back and forth. Even Guy had recovered sufficiently from his monstrous hangover to enjoy cutting the trail dust in his throat with a few swigs of whiskey.

Two of the campers who had joined them were musical and broke out guitar and harmonica to play until the lateness of the hour and the fatigue of traveling finally caught up with everyone.

The campfire flickered and snapped as it died down. The travelers quickly went to sleep in their blankets, contented to know they would be at their destination the next day. The three Texas Rangers, as tired and worn out as the rest, did not drift off into restful slumber at all. It took them a long time to manage to get some fretful napping.

A time of reckoning awaited them in Waco that next day.

Thirteen

Charlie Delano unexpectedly reined in, forcing his two companions to come to an abrupt halt.

"Hey!" Guy Tyrone exclaimed angrily. "Let a feller know what you're gonna do, huh?"

Charlie ignored the outburst. "Yonder it is, boys," the Ranger captain announced.

The town of Waco, Texas, loomed on the distant horizon, the outlines of its buildings fuzzy in the haze caused by a very warm, early morning sun.

Charlie Delano, Guy Tyrone, and Gideon Magee, a quarter of a mile away from the community's northern edge, sat on their horses, looking at the town.

"Let's get out of folks' way here on the road," Gideon suggested. "We don't want to attract a lot of attention to ourselves anyhow." They rode a few yards off into the brush.

"We got a tough job to do," Guy said, echoing everyone's feelings.

Gideon filled his pipe and lit it. He puffed thoughtfully for a few moments. "Anybody got any ideas about how we're gonna handle this? Like you, maybe, Charlie, since you're in charge."

"Yeah. We can't go in there in the blind," Guy remarked. "That's for damn sure."

"Well, pards, look at it this way," Charlie suggested. "We don't know how many banks is in the town, we don't know which one the gang is gonna hit, we don't know which direction they're coming in from, and we don't know if the local law or somebody in the bank is helping 'em out."

Gideon puffed on his pipe. "By God, Charlie, you sure make us sound dumb."

"Maybe we are," Guy said, grinning. "At least for getting into a situation like this."

"We ain't dumb," Charlie said. "We're ignorant. Dumb means you can't learn nothing. Ignorant just means you don't know all about something. But it don't mean you can't get savvy real pronto."

"Well, we better get savvy or we're gonna get shot," Gideon pointed out. "And prob'ly from more'n one direction too."

"We'll drift in there one at a time," Charlie said. "I'll hit the main street and ride all the way up and back. Gideon, you take the side streets to the north as we go in. Guy, take the south. And keep low in case any of the gang has gone in there ahead o' the others. Once we're in, we'll scout out any banks we find. After we go all the way to the edge of the place, we'll turn around and come back to meet on this side o' town."

"I'll go in first," Guy said.

"Go on, then," Charlie told him. "But remember what I said. Keep your hat pulled down low."

"I gotcha." Guy nodded a good-bye, then urged his horse into a walk. He went back onto the road and turned toward town.

After five minutes, Charlie said, "Your turn, Gideon."

"See you later," Gideon said.

Charlie watched him go back to the road. Ten minutes passed before the Ranger captain flipped the reins, getting his own mount into motion. Charlie reached the road and made a turn toward Waco. He rode easily as a drifter would, seeming to be in no particular hurry to any casual observer. But his eyes took in everything as he surveyed the surroundings.

He reached the town limits and went through an outlying residential neighborhood made up mostly of dilapidated shacks and old adobe huts. When he reached the main street he went straight up the dirt thoroughfare. He passed two banks within a couple of blocks of each other and continued down the length of the rustic avenue.

When he reached the end, he turned and went around a cluster of corrals and livery barns before turning back to meet the others.

Going back through the town from another angle gave him a slightly different perspective on the appearance of the banks. Both were on corners rather than in the middle of other businesses. That made it easier to get to them and easier to make a getaway. When he reached the ragtag neighborhood he found Guy and Gideon waiting for him.

"Did you fellers find anything on the side streets?" Charlie asked.

"No banks on my side," Guy reported.

"And none on mine," Gideon said.

"The only banks in town is them two on the main street, then," Charlie surmised. "So the gang has got to hit either one of 'em."

"Or both of 'em," Gideon pointed out. "It appears to me that they're both easy targets."

"I noted that," Charlie remarked.

"Are we gonna bring in the local law?" Guy asked.

"Do you want to?" Charlie inquired.

Guy grinned sheepishly. "Since we don't know if we can trust 'em or not and the governor o' Texas might deny we're on his payroll, I reckon we're gonna have to face up to this one alone."

"That's the fact o' the matter," Charlie said.

"I know another fact," Gideon said. "Once the shooting starts, the local starpackers ain't gonna know bandit from Ranger."

"And neither will the local citizens," Charlie added. "Not that they would care much one way or the other from the way things is gonna appear to them."

Guy chuckled. "Now you two son of a bitches know what I been going through."

"What're we gonna do, Cap'n?" Gideon said as a way of letting it be known he didn't have the slightest idea of how to handle the dangerous situation. If he could have his way, he would simply ambush the gang out on the road before they reached town and shoot them all out of the saddle.

"Well," Charlie mused. "We got to keep out o' sight. Particularly Guy, since they know what he looks like. When the bank holdup starts, we got to be ready to move in fast with our shooting irons blasting."

"Yeah," Gideon said in way of agreement. "I wouldn't take the time to introduce ourselves."

"Are we gonna hit 'em before or after they do their business?" Guy asked.

"We can only do it after," Charlie said. "There ain't no law against 'em walking into the bank.

The legal twist is when they come out with the money. And since I don't think they're gonna be making withdrawals on their own accounts, I'll assume what they done was illegal. So we can shoot 'em down without worrying about getting ourselves in trouble." He was thoughtful for a few moments. "Did either o' you find a good place to hunker down and wait on the side streets?"

"I did," Gideon said. "There's an old lean-to that's about to topple over. I reckon if a feller decided to rest there a bit out o' the sun, he wouldn't attract too much attention."

"Let's hope that feller ain't fallen asleep when the shooting starts," Guy said.

"Don't worry about that," Gideon said. "When I got a chance to put some slugs into bad hombres, I'm just plumb too excited to sleep."

"Too excited or too happy?" Charlie asked.

"A little o' both, I reckon," Gideon said with a wink.

Charlie looked at Guy. "Any place on the other side for you to lay low?"

"Sure," Guy said. "I seen a narrow place between a coupla buildings across the street from them banks. There's room for two. I'm gonna have to stay back in the shadows so's they won't see me."

"Good," Charlie said. "In that case, we'll both wait there. I'll stay up near the street to keep an eye out. When I see 'em I'll whistle."

"Will you know 'em?" Guy asked. "You only got quick glimpses of 'em while you was shooting at 'em over my head."

"I seen 'em real good while they was chasing you, remember?" Charlie said. "Anyhow, I'll whistle out a coupla times good and loud. That shouldn't attract any special attention. It'll just sound like some feller calling a pal or his horse or dog."

"Let's get to it, then," Gideon suggested. "Erickson's boys could be here in an hour or two."

"If this is the day," Charlie pointed out.

"It is," Guy said confidently. "I learned something about their timing. When Gustavo Fairweather shows up with a job, he means right away."

"That makes sense," Charlie allowed. "Setting it up too far in advance is asking for trouble when you're depending on bribery for your information." He patted his six-gun. "Let's get into position, boys. We'll be hard at work before we know it."

The three Rangers moved to their posts in the same manner they'd entered the town, one at a time. Slowly and nonchalantly, they managed to move to the positions where they'd wait for the bank robbery without attracting any undue attention from the local citizenry.

Gideon went to the old lean-to and tied his horse to it. He sat down in the shade of the rickety shelter, appearing to be asleep. But every nerve in his body was tense and ready for action. Across the street, hidden back in the shadows of the narrow alley, Guy waited anxiously. Charlie Delano was close to the street, able to observe all the comings-and-going on Waco's principal business avenue.

The first hour was exciting because of the anticipation of the gang's arrival. But as the second slipped past the midway point, the Rangers started to get restless. Charlie's neck got sore from looking up and down the street.

On the other side of the main thoroughfare, enjoying the shade under the lean-to, Gideon amused himself with thoughts of shooting outlaws into bloody heaps. Guy, having to keep himself back out of sight, began to doze off.

The third hour had barely begun when Charlie emitted a whistle.

Guy came awake. He went forward and peered carefully around Charlie out onto the street. A group of familiar-looking horsemen had appeared on the scene.

"That's them, all right," he said. "I see Ned Paulson in the front."

"Get ready," Charlie said. "There's Gideon across the way." He waved. "And he's ready."

"All we got to do is wait for 'em to hit one o' them banks," Guy said.

"Let's see which one it is," Charlie said. He reached back and gave Guy a shove. "Move into the shadows. I don't want none o' them bastards glancing over here and seeing you. If that happens, they'll know they rode into a trap."

"I'm gonna get my carbine," Guy said.

"Get mine while you're back there," Charlie said. "And do it pronto!"

Moments later Guy was back. He slipped Charlie's Winchester to him. "What's happening?"

"They went into the bank that's catty-cornered there," Charlie said. "Hang on now."

The gang was fast and professional. In less than ten minutes they were out of the bank, satchels and bags in hand as they rushed toward their horses.

Charlie stepped out and took aim, then fired.

Ned Paulson lurched sideways with a bullet in his neck.

Now Gideon went into action. He fired from a kneeling position at the side of the general store next to the bank. He hit one man with a killing shot, then dropped another by sending a slug into his knee.

"Aim higher, Gideon!" Guy shouted with a grin. He stepped out a couple of paces from the alley. "Hey, Ed Hall! Where are you?" He shot into the shocked group of bandits. One of them crumpled to the street.

The gang recovered from their surprise and began to fight back with vicious fusillades.

People on the street rushed inside stores and other buildings in a panic. Confused, frightened, and angry, the citizens peered out at the gunfight as they tried to figure out what exactly was going on.

Guy dove back into the alley as bullets kicked up spurts of dirt at his heels and slammed into the building around his head. "I think we riled 'em, Charlie!"

Charlie didn't reply. He began to shoot the gang's horses. The wounded animals neighed and whirled, causing confusion as they bumped into each other and bandits who tried to climb into the saddles of uninjured mounts.

A couple of the luckier robbers managed to break loose from the melee and get mounted up. They galloped down the street, low on their horses as they pounded out of town with bullets whipping the air around them.

"The son of a bitches got away!" Gideon yelled in rage.

"It's Elmer Sherman and Lee Fenney," Guy said as way of identifying them. "They'll ride all the way to Stavanger without stopping."

The people in the buildings, still unsure of what was really happening, stayed behind cover. The bank robbery had been so fast and smooth that none were aware of its occurrence. All they could perceive were two groups of men shooting furiously at each other right in the middle of the day in the business district.

Seeing Sherman and Fenney escape caused Charlie, Guy, and Gideon to redouble their efforts to stop the rest of the gang. They increased their fire, pumping the cocking levers of the carbines and firing almost without aiming into the now lessening numbers of the gang.

While the gun battle raged, the local sheriff and his one deputy on duty made valiant efforts to gain control over the situation. They dodged and weaved their way between buildings and other cover near the scene of the battle, being careful to keep out of harm's way as they approached the flying bullets. But they were as confused as the rest of Waco's citizens. Without knowing the bank had been robbed, the lawmen didn't have the slightest idea what the fight was about.

Finally, both reached a decision that it wasn't an attack on the town. They pulled back to see what was going to happen—or who would survive the flying bullets.

By then all the bandits were down dead or wounded. The money they'd robbed lay in its containers among the human debris that was left of the gang. As suddenly as its explosive beginning, the gunfight ended abruptly.

Now the street was silent in its aftermath.

Charlie waved at Gideon, signaling him to head out of town past the lean-to where he had waited. The Ranger captain gestured that he was to head north. He turned to Guy. "Let's you and me get out the opposite way. We'll meet Gideon on the Dallas side of this town."

The trio of Rangers made a quick, silent escape from the scene. They left the citizens of Waco, at least for the moment, still unaware that not only had their bank been robbed, but the robbery broken up.

Minutes after the Rangers left, the citizens came out onto the street and cautiously approached the corpses and wounded that lay piled up in front of the bank.

"Well, I'll be damned!" one said as he finally figured it out when he spotted the money bags. "Them galoots robbed the bank."

"Who was them others that shot 'em up?" another wanted to know.

The sheriff and his deputy joined the crowd. The senior lawman looked at his subordinate and shrugged.

"I don't even want to think about writing up a report on this."

"How can we?" the deputy asked. "We don't even know for sure what happened!"

Fourteen

The atmosphere in Ace Erickson's office was tense as he drummed his fingers on the desktop. The outlaw boss looked across the oaken expanse of the piece of furniture at the somber features of Elmer Sherman and Lee Fenney. A few feet away, Gustavo Fairweather stood by the door. He, too, was irritable and upset.

"And you both saw this fellow named Guy Tyrone shooting at you there in Waco?" Ace asked them.

"We sure did, Mr. Erickson," Sherman said. "We know him good, don't we, Lee?"

"Yeah," Fenney answered. "The son of a bitch was a friend o' Jess Garbel's. They was supposed to have been in jail together or something."

The lawyer Maxwell Banter sat at one side of the desk. He showed his own irritation by short, shallow puffs on his cigar. "One of the new fellows told you that Tyrone was a Texas Ranger, is that right?"

"Yes, sir," Fenney said.

"What was this new fellow's name?" Banter asked.

"I don't recollect his name 'cause I never seen him before," Fenney said. "And I don't reckon I'll see him again since Guy Tyrone shot him full o' holes there in Waco."

"Do you recall when that fellow accused Guy Tyrone of being a Texas Ranger?" Banter wanted to know.

Fenney nodded. "That was when Gustavo had brung him and the others out to the ranch. When the new feller—"

Fairweather interrupted. "The man's name was Ed Hall."

"Yeah," Fenney said. "I remember now. Anyhow, when this Ed Hall seen Tyrone, he had a fit. He said he seen Guy get swored into the Rangers right in front o' him after beating him up with a club and throwing him in jail."

Sherman got into the conversation. "So after this new feller says that, Tyrone throwed down on us and was off that ranch like a bat out o' hell. We follered after him, but a whole passel of other hombres bushwhacked us and we had to get out o' there."

Gustavo Fairweather was more certain. "I figger there was between three to six of 'em. But they was in good cover, so they coulda been less if they was moving around and shooting at us from differ'nt places."

Ace Erickson lit a cigar. "Can you boys think of anything else about this Guy Tyrone to tell us?"

"I reckon not, Boss," Fenney said.

"Well, thanks, boys," Ace said. "You go on out there to the bar. I told the barkeep and the gals that you're not supposed to get charged a dime for enjoying yourselves."

"Well, thank you kindly, Mr. Erickson," Sherman said. "But it seems ever' time I turn around lately, I'm getting bushwhacked. And after what I been through the last coupla days, I just want to get a bottle and go off in a corner someplace and get good'n drunk."

"Me too," Fenney said, echoing his partner's feelings.

"Suit yourselves, boys," Ace said. "And don't worry. We're going to straighten this out. Things will be good for us again like they were before."

"I sure hope so," Fenney said.

Fairweather opened the door and let the two outlaws out. He walked to the desk and sat down. "We're up against something big. I can tell you that."

"The situation is most unusual," Ace said. "According to the Waco newspaper, the bank had been robbed and somebody ambushed the robbers in a quick but bloody shoot-out. Then, instead of sticking around and sorting things out like normal law officers would, the men—both number and identity unknown—simply disappeared, leaving corpses and the bank money to be gathered up by the townspeople."

"It's strange, all right," Fairweather said.

Ace looked at Banter. "I hope you're looking into this."

"Of course I am," Maxwell Banter said. "It's possible that certain elements in the governor's office instigated some sort of action. If so, it would be very difficult for my contacts to inform me of the situation in a timely manner."

"They could do something on their own, couldn't they?" Ace asked.

"Yes, but it would take them some time," Banter said. "But to be sure, I've got to tap the correct source. We've got money out in a lot of parts of the Texas state government and law enforcement, but that doesn't mean everyone we're paying off knows all the answers. It's going to be a puzzle that needs putting together. I've sent some telegrams out. Some answers should be coming in starting today."

"That botched-up Waco job cost us more than twenty-five thousand dollars," Ace pointed out. "Add that to the train we lost, and there are some sons of bitches that owe us a lot. I mean to collect."

"We've got to round up some more pistoleros," Fairweather said. "Right now we only got two men. That ain't hardly enough to pull candy out of a baby's hand."

"We have *three* men," Ace corrected him. "You're riding with the gang now, Gustavo. I can't trust anyone else to take over in a situation like this."

Fairweather sighed. "I kinda expected that ever since Ned Paulson got shot."

"You've got to take charge of the troops in the field," Banter said.

"Well, that's fine with me," Fairweather said. "There's nothing I'd enjoy more than pumping some .45 slugs into certain Texas Rangers I could mention."

"You'll get your chance," Ace assured him.

"We'll make sure you have more than a chance," Banter said. "We'll be able to find out exactly who they are."

"I got my suspicions that it was them Rangers that got rid o' Grogan and his boys," Fairweather said. "If they'd rode off to rustle some government horses, they'd been back at least a coupla weeks ago. And if they'd got caught, we'd heard about it. I think they're out there buried someplace on that ranch."

A light tapping at the door sounded and Dinah Walters came in. She frowned in puzzlement. "What's the matter with those two fellows? They don't have any interest in my girls at all. They're just sitting at a corner table mumbling to each other and drinking whiskey as fast as they can."

Ace smiled. "Let me tell you something, my darling. If there was ever a hell on earth, those two have seen it. I don't know what the Texas Rangers have unleashed on us, but it's going to take everything we've got to put things back the way we want them."

"That's right," Banter agreed. "We'll have to pay out plenty of money in the right places—"

Fairweather interrupted. "And put bullets in the right bellies."

"Where is the rest of the gang?" Dinah asked. She wondered about the man she'd met named Guy Tyrone.

"All dead," Fairweather said. "Those that didn't get lead poisoning at the train robbery is in the cold ground in Waco's boot hill."

Dinah felt a stab of grief and regret. "Oh!"

"Is something the matter?" Ace asked.

"It's a shock," Dinah said. "I just never expected anything like that to happen." She nervously cleared her throat. "I mean, things were going just the way you wanted them to, Ace. Plenty of money was rolling in and there wasn't a bit of trouble."

"Well, there's one feller and his pals to thank for this latest bad luck," Fairweather said. "Do you remember that hombre that came in here with Ned Paulson after the gang tried to take that train?"

Dinah, suddenly hopeful, tried to be nonchalant. "I'm not sure."

"His name was Guy Tyrone," Fairweather said. "Now do you know who I'm talking about?"

"Yes. I remember him," Dinah said. A picture of Guy's handsome face flashed through her mind.

"Well, he's a Texas Ranger," Fairweather said. "And him and his Ranger pals bushwhacked us at Waco yesterday."

"He's alive?" Dinah asked.

"Not for long," Fairweather said coldly.

Further conversation was interrupted when the bartender stepped through the door with an envelope. "This came from the Western Union office for Mr. Banter." He walked over and handed it to the lawyer. "Lee and Elmer is so drunk out there they're crying in their liquor."

"They've been scared witless," Ace said. "Give them anything they want. And, don't forget, it's on the house."

"Yes, sir." The man went back to his work.

Maxwell Banter opened the telegram and read it. "This is interesting."

Fairweather leaned forward. "Does it tell about the Rangers they sent after us?"

"Not here," Banter said. "They can't put something like that in a telegram. Everybody would know they'd sent us information. This is a kind of code I devised with Judge Bacon. He says here that my cousin is coming to visit with news from home and should be here today. All that means is that a special messenger is coming with the information we need."

Ace looked at Dinah. "You might as well go on out to the bar and mind your girls. We won't be doing anything very interesting in here."

"Sure, Ace," Dinah said. "Are you sure that fellow Guy Tyrone who came in here with Ned is a Texas Ranger?"

"We certainly are," Ace answered.

"And he's alive?" Dinah asked.

Fairweather looked at her. "Does that make you happy?"

She laughed nervously. "Of course not. Why should it? I just couldn't figure out how or why he would do such a crazy thing."

Banter said, "That's something we'll know before too many more days have gone by."

"And we'll put a stop to it," Ace said.

"Well," Dinah said. "Good luck, boys." She left the office.

Gustavo Fairweather stood up. "I ain't gonna get much done sitting around here. I'll need two or three days to round up the hired guns we need. But I ain't taking 'em to Grogan's ranch. The Texas Rangers will be thick as fleas on a hound in summer around there."

"Do you have any plans where to hole up?" Ace asked.

"Yeah," Fairweather said. "It ain't comfortable,

but it'll be safe enough. It's a line camp just north over the Cooke County line."

"It's not too far out of the way, is it?" Ace asked.

"We'll be handy, boss," Fairweather assured him. "Don't worry none about that."

"We'll see you when you get back," Ace said.

Fairweather, never one to stand on ceremony, left them without another word. After he'd gone, Banter sank into deep thought. "I have a suggestion on how to run this new gang," Banter said. "Consider it advice from your lawyer."

"That's how you earn your split from the take," Ace said. "What's your idea?"

"Maybe I could pull something and turn those Texas Rangers that have caused us so much grief into wanted men," Banter said.

"How the hell could you do that?" Ace asked interested.

"It's a matter of getting warrants issued," Banter said. "A tricky job, but not impossible."

"But that would mean other Texas Rangers would be sent to hunt them down," Ace said. "Do you think they would do it?"

"Orders are orders," Banter said. "And if legal warrants are issued, they wouldn't have any choice." He shrugged. "Besides, there's been a Ranger or two in the past that went bad. It wouldn't be anything new."

"You're right," Ace said with a smug grin. "What irony! Texas Rangers shooting and killing other Texas Rangers."

"That's about it," Banter said.

Ace continued to smile. "Just for being such a

smart fellow, I think I'll break out a good bottle of brandy for you."

"It's been a long time since I enjoyed a snifter of brandy," Banter said.

Ace got up and walked to the liquor cabinet. He opened it and pulled out a squat, round bottle. He turned and showed it to Banter. "How does that look?"

"My God!" Maxwell Banter said. "That's Cherente brandy!"

"It just came in yesterday," Ace said. "I ordered it for you quite a while back." He took the liquor to the desk and set it down. "I think we both deserve a taste of the best."

"It will help the time pass while we wait for the messenger," Banter said, pleased.

Ace went back to the liquor cabinet and returned with two snifters and a box of cigars. "These are the best—Havana Supremas. Good liquor and good tobacco."

"Allow me to correct you," Banter said. *"Excellent* liquor and *excellent* tobacco."

The two settled down to enjoy the delights of superior smoking and drinking. They drifted into small talk as the evening eased by.

Finally, toward ten o'clock, the bartender rapped on the door again. He opened it. "A man out here has a message for you, Mr. Banter."

"Send him in," Banter said.

A dusty traveler, weary and saddle-sore, walked into the office. He nodded politely to Ace. "Howdy, Mr. Erickson."

"How are you this evening, Jack?" Ace asked.

"I'm tuckered," Jack replied. "I've rode hard all the

way from Dallas." He approached Banter and handed him an oilskin pouch. "I was told to put this direct into your hands and no others, Mr. Banter."

"And so you have, Jack," Maxwell Banter said. "Good job."

"Go outside and treat yourself to an evening of drinking on me," Ace said. "You can join Lee Fenney and Elmer Sherman out there."

"I seen them two, Mr. Erickson," Jack said. "They're passed out with their heads on the table."

"Just ignore them and enjoy yourself," Ace said.

"I thank you kindly," Jack said happily. "I could sure use a few slugs o' rye." Anxious for refreshments, he made a hurried exit.

Banter opened the pouch and pulled out several folded sheets of paper. He spread them out on the desk and began reading.

Ace Erickson languidly smoked his cigar and took occasional, appreciative sips of the good brandy.

Finally, Banter looked up. "I can't believe there're only three of them."

"Three?" Ace asked.

"Yeah," Banter said. "Governor Coke has assigned three Texas Rangers the task of wiping out you and our entire operation."

"Do you have their names?" Ace asked.

"The one in charge is Captain Charlie Delano," Banter said. "He's a veteran of the Rangers. The other two were only recently sworn into the force."

"That coincides with that fellow's accusations against the man who rode with my gang," Ace said. "Guy Tyrone."

"Guy Tyrone was a deputy sheriff in Sweetwater before Delano brought him in on this case," Banter said.

"Who's the third?" Ace asked.

"A deputy U.S. marshal on a leave of absence," Maxwell Banter said. "His name is Gideon Magee."

"All that is in the message?" Ace asked.

"Yeah," Banter replied. "That's why we make payoffs, Ace. To have the contacts we need when we must be fully and correctly informed. This information is a bit late, unfortunately."

"Why is that?" Ace asked.

"It comes from a high source," Banter explained. "That makes it harder to send out." He read some more of the message. "There is also some information that will lead us to the solution I am seeking."

"I'm all ears, Maxwell," Ace said.

"These three are operating outside the law in a shadowy context," Banter said. "No doubt to protect the people who are after you. If you become a political power in this state, nobody wants you to know they tried to bring you down."

"Then we can follow your idea and put the law on them," Ace said happily.

"And it won't take long, Ace," Banter said.

"Are you sure about that?" Ace asked.

"Of course," Banter said. "Those three are already outside the law. The writer of this letter has the authority and necessary connections to put that interfering trio on a wanted list. I will write him immediately and tell him to issue warrants for their arrests."

Ace laughed. "So now the Texas Rangers are going to be hunting them down, hey?"

"True," Maxwell Banter said. "Our troubles are practically over."

"And theirs is just beginning," Ace said.

Banter chuckled. "They're dead men and just don't know it."

Ace laughed and raised his brandy glass. "Here's to the Texas Rangers, God bless 'em!"

"And to three in particular," Maxwell Banter echoed. "Delano, Tyrone, and Magee—God *damn* 'em!"

Fifteen

Guy Tyrone idly poked at the glowing coals in the fire. With Charlie Delano away, only he and Gideon Magee occupied the campsite. Charlie Delano had been unexpectedly called back to Dallas to report to Pascal Bond without delay.

Guy glanced up at his companion, who chewed softly on the unlit pipe in his mouth. Guy shook his head. "It don't make sense."

"Doing things the official way never does," Gideon said. "Don't worry none about it."

"But we could've gone to Stavanger and wiped out Ace Erickson and Gustavo Fairweather and anybody else that wanted to take us on," Guy protested. "As far as we know, we'd only have to draw down on Erickson and Gustavo."

"That's about right," Gideon agreed.

"Then how come we couldn't?" the younger lawman demanded to know. "I thought that was the plan."

Gideon pointed his pipe at his companion to emphasize the point he was about to make. "One thing you'll learn if you ever stop packing a star in small towns and get into state or federal law enforcement is that there's rules and orders and regulations that has got to be followed. And that's particularly important when instructions on a case is give to you. You do what you're told. Just like a good soldier."

"Well, Charlie should've ignored them orders to report in to that feller Pascal Bond in Dallas," Guy said angrily. "We coulda cleaned up Stavanger, then gone to Bond and say we didn't get his message."

"But we did get his message," Gideon said.

"We could've lied about it," Guy said.

Gideon shook his head. "You're a goddamned Texas Ranger and you got to obey orders. There's plenty I never liked doing as a U.S. deputy marshal, but I did what had to be did as part o' my job." He pulled out his tobacco pouch. "The little things you do as a sheriff don't matter nothing outside the town you serve. But when you're part of a big organization, you got to put your own wants and opinions second." He filled the pipe.

"Why?" Guy asked. "Just tell me that."

"Mainly on account of you don't know the overall situation," Gideon said. "So you figger the folks telling you what to do know more about things than you do."

"What if you see some feller that needs shooting and you been told not to shoot him?" Guy asked.

"Then I wouldn't shoot him," Gideon said.

"Haw!" Guy crowed. "I don't believe that! You got the itchiest trigger finger of anybody I've ever knowed."

"Oh, yeah?" Gideon argued. "A coupla years back I was told not to shoot ol' Red Buck Olson under no circumstances. And I didn't. When I come across him, I got sneaky and caught him in his camp at night. I brung him in alive and kicking." He puffed his pipe again. "And it was a good thing I done it that way too. It turned out he was wanted as a witness on a special case that I didn't even know about."

"Aw!" Guy said.

"See?" Gideon emphasized. "There's always a reason for orders." He laughed. "It might be a stupid reason, but it's a reason just the same."

"I reckon I ain't cut out for big organizations, then," Guy said testily. "When this case is over, I'm getting out o' the Rangers and heading back for a town job somewheres." He angrily poked at the fire, sending up a shower of sparks. "When is Charlie supposed to be back, anyhow?"

"I'm expecting him to show up pretty quick," Gideon said. "He's already had plenty o' time to ride to Dallas, jaw with Pascal Bond, then come on back."

"Maybe he got drunk and went up to a room with a dancehall gal," Guy said.

"Maybe he did," Gideon allowed.

"Maybe he's whooping and yelling and dancing the fandango," Guy said.

"Maybe he is," Gideon repeated.

Charlie Delano's voice broke in from the brush. "And maybe he's sneaking up on two of the dumbest bastards in Texas."

"Maybe he is," Guy hollered out. "It's about time you got back."

Charlie strode into camp leading his horse. "Don't you two know nothing about posting a lookout?"

"A lookout?" Guy asked. "We just shot hell out o' the Ace Erickson gang. Who do we got to look out for? Their ghosts?"

Charlie went about hobbling his horse. When he finished, he joined the other two at the fire. He looked into the empty pot sitting beside the flames. "What'd you two have?"

"Pinto beans and tortillas," Guy said.

"Did you eat it all? Couldn't you save any for me?" Charlie asked.

Guy smirked. "Don't expect us to believe you come up here from Dallas with an empty belly, Charlie Delano. Not with all them restaurants and pretty waitresses all over the place."

Charlie grinned. "I just wanted you to feel guilty."

"Well, we ain't feeling guilty, so you can forget all about it," Guy said.

"Speaking of Dallas," Gideon said. "What'd you learn down there?"

"Yeah!" Guy snapped. "And how come they called us off from going to Stavanger?"

"Because the secret of our mission is over," Charlie said. "Fact o' the matter is, we're gonna be joining up with some other Rangers for a raid on Stavanger later this afternoon."

"Good," Gideon said. He looked at Guy. "See what I mean about following orders? There was a reason for Pascal Bond holding us back."

"We still could've cleaned up Stavanger on our own by now," Guy insisted.

"Damnation! Stop bellyaching!" Gideon said. "Let's get this job over with so's I can get back to tracking no-good son of a bitches in the Indian nations."

"And I can get a nice, quiet uncomplicated job as a town deputy somewheres," Guy said.

"Don't you want to be the sheriff?" Gideon asked.

Guy shook his head. "Nope. Too much worry. I'll take the deputy's job."

"Suit yourself," Gideon said. He glanced at Charlie. "Where are we gonna meet these other Rangers?"

"At a place southeast of Decatur," Charlie said. "I know where it is."

"Decatur!" Guy exclaimed. "Hell, we're gonna have to leave now if we want to get there in time to hit Stavanger."

"That's right," Charlie said. "Why do you think I didn't unsaddle my horse." He looked over at his friends' mounts. "If I was you two, I'd throw some heavy leather over them cayuses."

Gideon got to his feet and knocked the burning tobacco out of his pipe. "Let's break camp, Guy."

"Sure," Guy said standing up.

"How many Rangers are we gonna team up with?" Gideon asked, beginning to pack his gear.

"About six, I reckon," Charlie said. "Pascal Bond wasn't too sure."

Guy, being lighter and more nimble than Gideon, was packed and ready to ride out a good five minutes ahead of the burly lawman. While he waited, he said, "Now that we're getting closer to finishing out this case, I want you both to understand that I meant what I said before."

"What are you talking about?" Charlie asked.

"I'm keeping the loot I got in them robberies," Guy said. "And I don't want nobody telling me no."

"We never said you couldn't," Charlie assured him.

"Yeah. But Gideon here is talking about stupid orders and rules and regulations in big organizations like the Rangers," Guy said.

"They won't even take that into consideration," Charlie said.

"That's only fair," Guy went on. "After all, I did earn it, didn't I? It was my cut o' the take on them robberies."

Charlie said, "The state o' Texas is gonna be so glad to be rid of Ace Erickson, they're prob'ly even gonna give us a reward."

"A big one?" Guy asked.

"Are you joshing?" Charlie asked with a laugh. "What makes you think you're gonna get rich in the Texas Rangers?"

"Nothing. 'Specially since I seen what a poor, starving son of a bitch you are," Guy mumbled. He shook a finger at Gideon. "C'mon! Let's go!"

"I'm ready," Gideon announced. He climbed up into the saddle. "Lead the way, Charlie."

"Here we go, boys," Charlie said, mounting his horse. "We got a showdown to get to."

"You mean *another* showdown," Guy said.

The three Rangers rode out of the camp area and headed northeast across open country toward the rendezvous point near Decatur. They rode steadily, keeping in mind that their horses would have to be fresh enough for the trip over to Stavanger for the final shootout with Ace Erickson and what was left of his organization.

Heavily-armed and determined, their initial bantering and joking slowly came to a stop as they neared the place where they would join up with the others. The trio was moving into one of the most dangerous situations in frontier law enforcement—hitting cornered outlaws. Warrants, legal directives, and judicial documents meant nothing at that point. From then on, all issues would be decided with guns and guts.

And that meant somebody was going to die.

Toward midafternoon they reached the road that ran between Decatur and Denton. Charlie led them into a westerly direction. "Let's press on, boys," he urged them. "We don't want to be late."

"You don't suppose they went without us, do you?" Gideon wondered.

"They better not have," Guy grumbled. "We put too much of ourselves into this job."

"Don't worry, boys," Charlie said. "Them other Rangers has got orders to wait for us."

Gideon looked at Guy. "See what I mean about orders? They prob'ly think what they been told is dumb, but they won't make a move 'til we get there."

"I would, if I was them," Guy said with a smirk. "I'd charge right into Stavanger and grab all the glory for myself."

"And that's why you'll never be no more than a town deputy after all this is said and did," Gideon said.

"Let's do more riding and less talking," Charlie said. "C'mon!"

They kept at a steady pace for another three-quarters of an hour when they saw the half-dozen men coming toward them. Charlie signaled a halt. He pulled his binoculars from their case and took a look.

"That's them, boys," he announced. "I recognize ol' Pete Dawson." He kicked his horse into a gallop with Guy and Gideon close behind. "Hey!"

Charlie yelled out. "Pete! Pete! It's me, Charlie Delano!"

The Rangers approaching hesitated a bit in what seemed to be shocked surprise. After a couple of moments they came back to life and responded to Charlie's yells of greeting by shooting at him.

"Hey!" Charlie bellowed in anger. "It's me, Charlie Delano, you stupid galoots!"

A yell came back from Pete Dawson. "I know it's you, goddamn your eyes, Charlie. Throw up your hands. I got a warrant for your arrest."

Charlie whirled his horse around, gesturing to Guy and Gideon. "Ride like hell, boys!"

Without asking questions or even consciously worrying about what was going on, Guy and Gideon followed him as Ranger bullets zipped through the air around their heads.

Charlie dashed along, bent low over his saddle while he pounded down the road. He went fifty yards beyond where he, Guy, and Gideon had first gotten onto the country thoroughfare. At that point they wheeled south. The trio headed for a wooded area they had skirted before. The Ranger captain quickly spotted an entrance into the cover of the trees and rode straight in, quickly dismounting.

Guy and Gideon crashed in behind Charlie, almost colliding with his horse. They dismounted and joined their leader, carbines in hand, up at the tree line. Within moments the Rangers chasing them appeared. Charlie fired over their heads.

"You damn fool!" Guy hissed. "You'll give us away."

"You just relax and let me handle this," Charlie said.

The Rangers pulled over toward the road and quickly took cover in a stand of boulders. They wasted no time in returning fire.

Charlie took a deep breath, then hollered, "Pete! Pete Dawson!"

The incoming shooting died down, then ceased.

"Charlie!" came back the call. "I hear you."

"I want a parley," Charlie yelled. "Ranger honor."

"You ain't a Ranger no more," Pete shouted back. "I got a warrant for your arrest and them two fellers with you."

"On what charges?" Charlie asked.

"Bank robbery, train robbery, murder," Pete replied in a loud voice.

Gideon looked at Charlie. "What the hell is going on?"

"I sure as hell don't know," Charlie said. "But I'm gonna find out."

"It sounds like more of them orders in a big organization," Guy said disdainfully.

Charlie decided to try again. He shouted, "Pete, you and me has knowed each other over a long period o' years. I want a parley. No shooting from either side."

Only silence greeted the request for several long moments. Then Pete yelled, "I'll parley with you, Charlie."

Charlie laid down his carbine and stripped off his gun belt, leaving it with the long gun.

"Are you loco?" Guy asked.

"They're old pards," Gideon said. "They trust each other."

"That's right," Charlie said. "No matter what happens, don't do nothing to Pete."

"Even if one o' them Rangers shoot you?" Guy asked.

"That's right," Charlie said.

"Don't worry, Charlie," Gideon assured him. "We won't."

Charlie stepped out of the cover of the trees and walked across the open area to a point midway between his companions and the Rangers' positions in the boulders.

Pete Dawson, also unarmed, walked slowly from cover and approached his old friend. He was a tall, rangy man who moved with a slight limp. When he arrived, he looked at him. "Well, Charlie. What the hell's going on?"

"That's what I would like to know, Pete," Charlie said. "I'm working on a case involving Ace Erickson over at Stavanger. I got orders to meet you at Decatur and we'd move against Erickson together."

"That ain't what I heard, Charlie," Pete said. "I heard you'd gone bad. They tell me that you and them two pals o' yours was gonna rob the bank at Decatur."

"What makes you think I took up robbing banks?" Charlie asked. "Along with trains and committing murder."

"A warrant I got," Pete said. "And special orders to get you one way or the other."

"Whose orders, Pete?" Charlie asked.

"Pascal Bond's," Pete replied. "Official agent for the governor who has General Steele's authority to issue orders to the Texas Rangers."

"Pascal Bond!" Charlie exclaimed. "That's who I'm working for. Hell, me and my two partners have wiped out Ace Erickson's gang. There ain't nothing between us and him."

"Then how come you didn't just go on into Stavanger and do him in?" Pete wanted to know.

"I got orders to meet you at Decatur, that's why!" Charlie angrily exclaimed.

"From who?"

"From that back-shooting, double-dealing, son of a bitch Pascal Bond!" Charlie cussed.

Pete was thoughtful for a few moments. "Charlie, I've knowed you for a long time. It could be you're in a hell of a mess brought on by some shenanigans of Ace Erickson or his lawyer."

"That's exactly the case," Charlie insisted.

"But on the other hand, maybe you've really gone bad," Pete said. "You wouldn't be the first lawman to do it. The Good Lord knows we don't get paid nothing worth shucks. More'n one star-packer has decided to get some extry cash for his old age."

"I'm asking for your trust on this, Pete," Charlie said.

"I already been thinking on that, Charlie," Pete said. "And I'm gonna make a deal with you."

"I appreciate that, Pete," Charlie said sincerely. Then he frowned. "What kind o' deal?"

"I'll give you three days to clear yourself and them pards you're riding with," Pete said. "Then me and my boys here are moving in on you hard and fast. And when we catch up with you, we ain't asking questions. It's shoot first, then sort out the mess."

"I need more'n three days," Charlie said. "We can't move around the country no more like we did before. You can be sure there's more'n one copy o' that warrant out."

"Three days," Pete said.

"I need a week, Pete!" Charlie insisted.

"Three days," Pete said again. "I'm taking a hell of a chance as it is. "If you get clean away, I can kiss this Ranger badge good-bye. And I might see the inside of the state prison too. But in or out o' jail, I'll come for you, Charlie. I don't take a wronging from no man."

"I understand," Charlie said. "And I appreciate the chance you're taking. I'll always be obliged to you, Pete."

"Three days," Pete Dawson said. He lifted his hand in farewell, then walked back toward the boulders where the other Rangers waited.

Charlie returned to the trees. He stepped back into their protective cover and sat down. "We got three days."

"Three days for what?" Guy asked.

"Three days to straighten things up and come out of this alive," Charlie said. "There's warrants out for us by name."

"That don't sound like enough time," Gideon said.

Charlie smiled weakly. "It ain't. But what're you gonna do?"

Guy laughed without humor. "Die trying."

Sixteen

Charlie Delano rode steadily, keeping his horse at a ground-eating canter while his companions, Guy Tyrone and Gideon Magee, trailed behind in impatient anticipation of what he had in mind.

They sensed their leader was deep in thought, working on a solution to their dangerous predicament. This was evident when Charlie had begun their trip away from the confrontation with the Rangers without a word of explanation. All he'd done was give a gruff signal to follow him, then lit out. That left Guy and Gideon completely in the dark about his intentions.

The three men followed a southerly route, staying west of Dallas, until Charlie made a sudden, unexpected turn eastward. He offered no accounting of the unanticipated action and ignored the questions that Guy shouted at him. Gideon, always willing to wait for answers, kept his impatience under control.

Charlie continued pressing on until the cloudy sky caused the evening's darkness to descend on them faster than usual. The sunlight, obscured by the heavy cover of high vapor, rapidly faded away. Only when the features of the ground were difficult to see did Charlie finally head for some trees growing along the bank of the Trinity River. He reined in abruptly and swung out of his saddle.

Guy came to a halt directly behind him. "How come we're stopping, Charlie?"

"I'm tired, ain't you?" Charlie said.

"I'm tired and riled," Guy said.

"And there's a chance one of our horses might stumble. Or ain't you noticed it's kinda hard to see," Charlie added.

Guy dismounted. "I ain't noticed a whole lot, since we been too busy riding like crazy men. But I'll allow that I'm as curious as a cat in a new barn about what kind of trail you're blazing for us."

Gideon joined them, also swinging himself out of the saddle. "My butt began to think my horse was growing out of it," he said.

"Let's make a cold camp," Charlie said. "No sense in advertising our whereabouts."

"I thought you made a deal with them Ranger pals o' yours back at Decatur," Guy said. "How come we got to stay in the dark?"

"Because if there's warrants out for us, other lawmen are gonna know about 'em too," Charlie told him. "What'll we do if some county sheriff or federal marshal stumbles across us?"

"I reckon you're right," Guy agreed reluctantly.

"I sure could use some coffee, though," Gideon remarked. That was his way of complaining.

"Me too," Charlie said. "But it ain't worth a fire."

"Nope," Gideon said in agreement.

The three wanted men quickly unsaddled their mounts and set up camp. They were careful to hobble their horses within the confines of the thickest group of trees to make sure the animals didn't wander away in the darkness. When it came time to spread out their bedrolls, they picked spots where both cover and concealment were available.

Charlie settled down on the ground and leaned against his saddle. "Three days," he said. "We got three days to straighten this mess out."

"That ain't much," Gideon mused.

"Yeah," Charlie said. "But that's all Pete Dawson would give us. Anyhow, I figger we ought to be grateful."

"I ain't ever been in a fix like this," Guy said, also making himself comfortable. "To tell you fellers the truth, I don't know what we can do in that amount o' time to get us out of this trouble."

"I reckon that was all we could get," Gideon said. "Still, it was pretty generous of your old pal."

"Yeah," Charlie said. "I suppose it was, under the circumstances."

"Would you have did the same for him?" Guy asked.

"Sure," Charlie replied without hesitation.

Guy scratched his head. "In the meantime, Charlie, you got any idea of what we should do?"

"Yep."

A few moments of silence followed.

Guy eyed him. "Well? Are you gonna tell us?"

"Yep."

"Maybe within the next three days?" Guy added.

"Within the next three minutes," Charlie said. "I'm been thinking it out and have to put the finishing touches on my ideas."

"You plan things good," Gideon said.

"Sure he does," Guy said. "Look what a fine mess we're in now, thanks to him dragging us into his planning."

"Hush up!" Charlie snapped. "I got to finish thinking."

Guy and Gideon wisely closed their mouths and waited.

Finally Charlie shifted a bit and took a deep breath before speaking. "We got to get our hands on that son of a bitch Pascal Bond."

"Just to shoot him?" Gideon asked. "Or is there another reason?"

"Another reason," Charlie answered. "He's got the answers of who is really behind this and where Ace Erickson's weak points are."

"We'll have to beat it out of him," Guy said.

"Does that bother you?" Charlie asked.

"Not in particular," Guy said.

Gideon shook his head. "If we capture him, he'll be happy to talk to us. I know that type. He's a sneaky bastard that works behind other folks' backs. Pascal Bond ain't the kind to stand up to another man."

"How he's gonna act with us ain't important now," Guy pointed out. "First we got to get our hands on him."

"That's right," Charlie said. "We'll go into the Windsor Hotel in Dallas and grab him."

"He don't live there," Guy reminded Charlie. "That's just where he meets folks to do business."

"Then we'll get him there," Charlie said. "That shouldn't be hard."

"When're we gonna do that?" Gideon asked.

"We'll lay low tonight and all day tomorrow until late afternoon," Charlie said. "We'll leave here so's we get into Dallas after dark. We go to the hotel and send a message to Bond, telling him to meet us there."

"Oh, you betcha!" Guy scoffed. "He's gonna rush right down all by hisself to meet the three of us, ain't he?"

"We ain't gonna use our own names, you dumb shit," Charlie snapped. "I'll come up with an idea. Don't worry about it."

"I hope so," Guy said.

"Well," Gideon said, stretching. "I'm gonna rest up. I got an idea that we won't be getting much sleep in the next couple of days or so."

"Prob'ly not," Charlie agreed. "But we're gonna have to keep watch tonight and all day tomorrow while we're in this camp. Two hours on and four hours off, 'til we leave."

"I ain't sleepy," Guy said. "I'll take the first shift."

"I'll go second," Charlie volunteered.

"Good," Gideon said, yawning. "Then I'll turn in." He grinned. "Or at least lay down and set my sombrero over my face. I ain't in a mood to get under a blanket even if I am dawg-tired.

Without any further conversation, the three fugitives settled down into a routine that would carry them through the night. They slept, ate cold food, spoke only as much as necessary, and took turns standing guard. Those activities carried them through that entire night and into the dawn.

Although it was all monotonous, the campsite was a nice one. The weather was good, and the lapping of the river against the bank was soothing and pleasant. If it hadn't been for the fact that every lawman in the entire state of Texas was on the lookout for them, the time camping there would have been quite pleasant.

After the dawn sun broke over the horizon and began its climb through the sky, the day drifted by slowly with no alarms. The noon sun directly overhead was extremely warm, giving them another strong hint of the hot summer to come. The daylight hours were slow and cumbersome, but eventually the shadows lengthened and the bright disk in the sky oranged up and began sinking toward the western side of the prairie.

Finally, Charlie announced, "Time to saddle up."

Guy and Gideon, glad to have something to do, quickly got to their feet and wasted no time in getting to their horses and preparing to leave the cover of the trees. Guy as usual was the first ready. He pulled his carbine from the saddle boot and slowly led his mount out of the trees into the open country.

"The coast is clear," he announced back at the two older men.

Charlie and Gideon rode out and joined him. Guy forked his saddle. The trio, without another word to each other, galloped off toward Dallas with Charlie once again in the lead.

As before, the three fugitives traveled at a steady, careful pace across the darkening countryside. They kept a sharp lookout, going well out of their way to avoid farm or ranch houses as they drew closer to their destination.

Darkness finally moved in over Texas, and the lights of Dallas danced along the horizon at the bottom of the night sky as Charlie, Guy, and Gideon pressed on. Now they were able to step up the pace, breaking into a canter when the first outlying buildings of the city came into view. These adobe structures were but one of many Mexican neighborhoods that spread out south from the metropolitan area.

Charlie held up his hand and brought their progress to a stop. "Let's wait out here for a couple of hours. I don't want to send for Pascal Bond 'til around ten o'clock."

Gideon glanced around. "I don't like the idea of being outside like this. We show up like a black cat on a snow-covered roof."

Guy licked his dry lips. "There's a cantina yonder."

"Let's wet our whistles," Charlie suggested.

It was a good place to bide their time. Close enough to be able to move in quickly without attracting undue attention, yet safe because no lawman would venture into the barrios unless in hot pursuit of an escaping criminal.

They dismounted outside a building that bore a sign proclaiming it as CANTINA EL GATO. Taking their carbines with them, they went inside. The Mexican customers turned to look at them and the glares were decidedly unfriendly.

Charlie grinned and dropped some money on the bar. *"Cerveza para todos,"* he announced in Spanish, letting the whole house know he was standing them all a round of beer.

The glares relaxed into grins, and the drinkers'

attention went back to themselves and the conversations that had occupied them before the gringos' entrance. The barkeep, happy there wouldn't be any trouble, set up the drinks.

The three wanted men settled around a table, getting a large pitcher of beer and three clay cups. Charlie poured each of them a cupful. He raised his. "Here's to better times ahead."

Guy and Gideon clinked their cups against his. Guy drank deeply, almost draining the container before he stopped. "That's good," he announced.

Gideon also treated himself to some deep swallows. He belched and rubbed his belly. "Well, Charlie. Are you gonna let us know what we'll be doing in another hour or so?"

"That's prob'ly a good idea," Charlie said.

"You figger on gunplay?" Guy asked.

"We got to avoid that at all costs," Charlie cautioned him. "Any shooting is gonna bring the law. That could mean Dallas starpackers and maybe a Ranger or two. We don't need that."

"Amen!" Gideon agreed.

"So I figger we'll go into the hotel and walk up to the desk clerk real bold like," Charlie said.

"We look kind o' grubby," Guy remarked.

Charlie shrugged. "We shouldn't have no trouble on account o' Pascal Bond has prob'ly been meeting with lots o' men off the trail."

"I just hope we ain't gonna be recognized," Guy said.

"We shouldn't," Charlie said. "And I'll write out a note and see that it's delivered pronto to Bond."

"What's the note gonna say?" Guy asked.

"I'm gonna ask him to meet us," Charlie said.

"And I ain't gonna use a name neither. I'll just sign it A.E. and G.F."

"What the hell is that supposed to mean?" Gideon asked.

"You can't figger it straight out, but Pascal Bond sure can," Charlie said. "He'll think them initials stand for Ace Erickson and Gustavo Fairweather."

The batwing doors of the cantina opened and several customers entered, going straight to the bar. Charlie eyed them carefully, nervously scratching his chin.

Guy was concerned. "Something the matter?"

"Yeah," Charlie said, lowering the brim of his hat. "One of them fellers is Chamaco Cortez. I throwed his ass in the calaboose down in Hidalgo 'bout three years ago."

"That was a long time back," Gideon said. "Maybe he's forgot about it."

Charlie shook his head. "Nope. He went to the penitentiary for a spell. And I'll bet he ain't been out long."

"Then he's mad," Guy said.

"Normally I wouldn't give a damn," Charlie said. "But I don't want to get all hung up here."

Guy asked, "What do you want to do?"

"Let's ease out o' here," Charlie said. "You two keep between me and the bar. Maybe he won't notice me."

Guy finished his beer. "I'm ready."

"Me too," Gideon echoed.

"Go on," Charlie told them. "But do it slow."

The three gringos carefully stood up, then moved slowly toward the exit with Charlie staying behind his pals. He kept his head down, looking away from the bar. When they reached the door, Charlie stepped ahead a couple of steps and went outside.

Guy and Gideon joined him. Guy chuckled. "That wasn't too bad."

"Let's ride," Charlie said.

They went to their horses and unlooped the reins from the hitching rack. Charlie slipped his foot into the stirrup.

A voice from the cantina shouted, "Charlie Delano! *Hijo de la chingada!*"

Charlie slapped leather and turned, coming up with a fire-spitting Colt. Both Guy and Gideon relied on their carbines as they blasted toward the cantina door.

Three Mexicans, their guns drawn, were rocked off their feet by the heavy impact of the slugs. The largest bounced from the building's wall and fell face forward to the dirt. He looked up and sneered, saying once again, *"Hijo de la chingada!"*

Charlie fired again, the bullet zapping across the open space and smacking straight into Chamaco Cortez's skull. Charlie spat. "I hate to be called a son of a bitch in any language."

"You're a sensitive man, Charlie Delano," Guy said, chambering another bullet.

More faces appeared at the door and a gun barrel showed up in the lantern light from the interior. Another fusillade from the gringos caused the small crowd to disperse.

"Ride!" Charlie yelled.

The trio vaulted into their saddles and kicked their horses into a mad gallop out of the neighborhood. They rode fast for fifteen minutes before Charlie slowed the pace down to a canter. Then he drew back on the reins more until his mount walked.

Guy looked back over his shoulder. "Reckon they'll foller us?"

Charlie shook his head. "Not into Dallas. But we sure as hell can't come back this way."

"I hope that little shoot-out ain't a sign of things to come," Guy remarked.

Gideon laughed without humor. "You can bet your ass it is, youngster."

"Well," Charlie said. "I never said this job was gonna be easy, did I?"

"You didn't say it was impossible neither," Guy countered.

"Let's go and get Pascal Bond," Charlie said. "We'll worry about what's gonna happen when it happens."

"Good idea," Gideon agreed.

"Speak for yourselves," Guy said. "I'm already fretting enough for all three of us."

Seventeen

Charlie Delano, Guy Tyrone, and Gideon Magee stepped up on the boardwalk in front of the Windsor Hotel in the center of Dallas's commercial district. The trio of wanted men paused long enough to give the downtown crowd a good looking over in case any lawmen they knew were among the passersby. Any chance meetings with starpackers would bring Charlie's plans to an abrupt, violent finish. But only shoppers, drinkers, and loafers dominated the scene.

"I sure ain't looking for no old friends," Gideon remarked dryly.

"Me either," Guy said.

The three men's horses, tied to a hitching rail down the street, stomped their hooves and blew through their nostrils after the quick gallop in from the city's outer edges.

It was a quarter after ten. The street lamps were lit, throwing a weak, yellow glare over the people moving along the street. Illumination from various businesses still open added a bit more luster to the city scene.

Charlie nodded to Guy. "Stay outside here and keep a sharp eye peeled," he instructed. "If you see anything that makes you nervous, ease on in the lobby. Or if there ain't time, just vamoose.

There's no sense in all of us getting shot up, so nobody will blame you none."

"I'll blame me, though," Guy said. "So I'll stick it out here one way or the other." He sauntered over to the front door of the hotel and leaned against it as if he were waiting for somebody.

"What am I supposed to do?" Gideon asked.

"Foller me in and watch the back o' the lobby," Charlie instructed. "I don't want any nasty surprises coming from that direction neither."

"Gotcha," Gideon said.

Charlie walked into the hotel with Gideon close behind. As he turned toward the front desk, he sensed Gideon moving on past him. Charlie went up to the desk clerk. "Howdy."

"Yes, sir?" the clerk asked. He was an experienced Texas hotel man. He knew that just because a fellow might look seedy and dusty from the open range didn't mean he wasn't important or didn't have money.

"I'm right anxious to get ahold o' Mr. Pascal Bond," Charlie said. "I understand you folks here at the Windsor can help me out."

"We certainly can," the clerk said. "We know Mr. Bond very well. He conducts a lot of his business in our meeting rooms."

"I'd be obliged if I could write him a note and have somebody deliver it," Charlie said.

"Yes, sir." The clerk retrieved a pen, ink bottle, and pad of paper from behind him. He hit the bell on his desk, calling out, "Front!"

A bellboy promptly presented himself, waiting for whatever instructions he would receive.

Charlie quickly wrote a message, then folded the

note in half. He slipped his hand into his pocket and got a silver dollar. Flipping it to the bellboy he said, "Boy, I want you to deliver this to Mr. Pascal Bond. Tell him he's got to be down here as quick as he can. It's important as hell." Charlie glanced at the desk. "Can we use that meeting room at the top of the stairs?"

"Yes, sir. It's available," the clerk said.

"That's where you'll bring him," Charlie ordered.

Happy with the generous tip, the bellboy touched a finger to his hat. "I'll take care of it right away, sir. Don't you worry none." He rushed off to tend to the errand.

Charlie nodded thanks to the clerk and slowly made his way up the stairs to the first landing. He went to the meeting room and slipped inside. A quick strike of a match lit a kerosene lantern. He kept it turned low as he settled down in a chair in the corner.

The fatigue of being chased and kept in a nervous state because of a dangerous situation settled in on Charlie Delano as he sat there. The fact that, legally, he was no longer a captain in the Texas Rangers rankled him inwardly too. He hadn't discussed it any with Guy and Gideon, but it bothered him considerably. That gloomy feeling was even stronger than the fear of facing death in the dangerous game they were playing. He dozed for short moments of time, coming instantly awake for a minute or two before relaxing again. His hand rested on his holstered pistol, ready for whatever might come through the door.

Twenty minutes after he'd gone into the room, Charlie heard a light rapping.

"Yeah," he said in a gruff whisper.

The portal opened and a slight, dumpy man stepped into the bleak light of the lantern. "Mr. Erickson?" Pascal Bond asked. "Gustavo?"

"Come on in," Charlie said, keeping his voice from being identifiable.

"Is that you, Gustavo?" Bond asked, closing the door.

"Yeah," Charlie whispered.

Bond walked toward him. "What's going on? I was sure surprised to—" He stopped as he drew close enough to recognize Charlie Delano. "Oh, my God!"

"Hello, Bond, you lying, conniving son of a bitch," Charlie said, quickly drawing his gun. He pointed the barrel at the frightened man's head. "I'm sure tempted to splatter your brains all over that far wall."

"What are you doing here?" Bond fearfully demanded to know.

"I'm here to solve a mystery," Guy said. "The mystery of how Ace Erickson is beginning to run the state of Texas from a goddamned saloon in the town of Stavanger."

Bond laughed nervously. "I was the one who gave you that assignment a while back. Remember?"

"Yeah. I remember," Charlie said. "And Pete Dawson tells me that you told him I was a wanted man. In fact, ol' Pete says you saw to it that warrants was put out on me, Guy Tyrone, and Gideon Magee."

"I don't have the power to issue warrants," Bond protested. "I couldn't do that."

"Maybe you can't, but the governor can," Charlie said. "And you can do a lot in his name if you want to." He shifted the Colt to his other hand. "The fact of the matter is, you got me and Guy and Gideon in a bad way. And I aim to get things set right one way or the other."

Bond said nothing, only licking at his dry lips.

Charlie continued. "That's why we sent for you, Bond. And we're gonna ask you some questions and we ain't gonna take no lying answers from you. Understand? We don't want to give Ace Erickson time to cover his tracks. I just figger on going after him and his pal Gustavo Fairweather without any more of a delay than is really needed."

Bond cleared his throat. "Well, do what you must."

"Oh, I will, Bond," Charlie said. "You can depend on that. By the way, did you come down here in a buggy?"

"No," Bond said. "I rode down on my mare."

"I reckon when you figgered that note was from Ace Erickson and Gustavo Fairweather, you didn't want to waste time hitching up a horse to a buckboard, did you?"

Bond ignored the question. "Well, what do you expect of me?" he asked.

"You're going with us," Charlie said. "And if you so much as blink an eye the way we don't like it, I'll guarantee you that three six-guns is gonna pump a total of eighteen Texas bullets straight into your fat carcass."

"I won't resist," Bond said. "You'll have no reason to want to harm me."

"No. I reckon I won't," Charlie said, getting to his feet. He sensed the very real fear in the man. "Now I'm gonna tell you what to do, and I'll expect you to act like a good li'l soldier and obey ever' order I give you." He motioned with the pistol. "Move on to the door and step through it. Then walk down the stairs and across the lobby. I'll be right behind you. Go out the front door and wait for my next instructions. Understand?"

"Yeah," Bond said.

"You say, 'Yes, sir, Cap'n Delano,' " Charlie hissed through clenched teeth.

"Yes, sir, Captain Delano," Bond dutifully repeated.

"Move on, then," Charlie said. He sighed. "I just wish we had time to order some of this hotel's Kentucky bourbon. Damn! That's good whiskey."

"I'm certain it is," Bond said testily. He walked toward the door and stepped through it with Charlie right behind him. Following instructions, he went down the stairs and walked across the lobby toward the front door.

Gideon Magee, toward the back of the hotel foyer, spotted the two. He moved after them, making it look like it was only a coincidence that he was leaving at the same time.

Charlie waved at the desk clerk. "Much obliged." He turned his attention to Pascal Bond. "Mind your manners and thank the man, Bond."

Bond nodded to the clerk. "Thank you."

Charlie guided his reluctant guest out the front door by gently pressing on his back. As they stepped out on the street, Guy Tyrone joined them.

"Where's your horse?" Charlie asked Bond.

"The speckled mare," Bond replied, pointing down the street.

"Now that's real handy," Charlie said. "He's right next to our cayuses."

Pascal Bond reluctantly led the group as they walked through the crowd. Knowing that any attempt at escape would result in three six-shooters pumping lead into him unnerved the man to the extent that he walked in a quick, jerky motion.

"Slow down!" Charlie hissed.

Guy hurried up beside Bond. He nudged him in the side with his elbow. "Don't look so damn unhappy, Bond. Smile."

Bond forced an insincere smile. When they reached the animals, he obeyed further instructions by waiting to mount his own horse until Guy and Gideon were in the saddle.

"Hop on," Charlie told him.

Bond slipped his foot into the stirrup. He took the reins after Charlie untied them and tossed them over the horse's head to him. For one wild moment he was tempted to make a gallop for safety, but Guy and Gideon quickly hemmed him in with their own animals.

Charlie nonchalantly got up into his own saddle. "Let's ride out of town, boys. To the west."

"Good idea," Gideon said. "I don't think it would be a good idea for us to ride back through that Mexican neighborhood."

Guy chuckled. "You mean *try* to ride back through it."

The group moved slowly down the street, keeping in close and forcing a couple of other riders to move out of the way. The pair started to protest the loss of what they considered the right of way, but close looks at the men they faced caused them to decide to just get out of the way without any remarks. Charlie sent Guy to take the lead while Gideon continued to closely flank Pascal Bond just behind him.

"Say, Pascal!" A call came from the crowd. "Pascal Bond!"

Guy, startled, glanced back at Charlie. The captain signaled a halt, then moved in closer to Bond. "Be careful what you say, or it'll be your life. I mean it, goddamn it!"

Bond swallowed hard and gave a half-hearted wave. "Evening, Ben."

"Evening, Pascal," said his friend. "And where might you be heading on such a fine spring night?"

"I, uh—I have some business," Bond said.

"You're the busiest dang man I've ever known," the other said. He paused. "You look down in the mouth. Are you feeling well?"

For a desperate moment, Bond felt the desire to cry out for help. But a warning hiss from Charlie Delano was enough to make him give up the idea. Bond shrugged. "I'm tired. That's all."

"Well, take care of yourself," the man advised him. "And say hello to Mildred for me."

"I'll do that," Bond replied. The other man moved on into the crowd. Bond said, "Was that good enough for you?"

"It was plumb fine," Charlie said. "Who's Mildred?"

"My wife," Bond answered.

Guy poked his arm. "Well, Pascal Bond, if you ever want to lay eyes on Mildred again, you'd best do exactly as we tell you, understand?"

"I understand," Bond said. Then he added, "Perfectly."

Charlie, Guy, and Gideon continued down the street with their unhappy guest. The crowd thinned considerably as they passed out of the commercial district and rode into Dallas's outlying residential sections.

"Turn north," Charlie whispered up to Guy as they reached a corner.

Guy did as he was told, leading them up a street that grew progressively darker. Finally spaces between the houses grew wider and wider until the group was in the open country of the prairie.

"Are we going anywhere in particular?" Guy asked.

"Just keep riding," Charlie instructed. "I know a place up here where there's a patch of woods where questions can be asked."

Gideon reached over and grabbed Bond's collar, shaking him hard. "And answered," he added.

Eighteen

Pascal Bond stood within the shadows of the trees, surrounded by his three captors. Bright moonlight streamed in through the branches overhead, eerily lighting not only the scene, but the solemn, angry faces of Charlie Delano, Guy Tyrone, and Gideon Magee.

Bond was frightened.

More frightened than he had ever been in his life. He knew he faced an interrogation in which evasiveness or hesitation on his part would be met with sudden, violent, painful, physical retribution. Pictures of being tortured Indian-style with fire flitted through his mind.

Charlie Delano was an expert in such situations. A cunning judge of human weaknesses, he chose the right moment and threw the punch with speedy deliberation. He aimed his fist to collide with Bond's cheek just below the left eye. The force of the unexpected punch turned the man a quarter turn. At that point he received a heavy, open-handed slap from Gideon Magee that kept the momentum of the rotation moving. That brought him face-to-face with Guy Tyrone, who threw a bolo punch straight to Bond's abdomen.

The victim doubled over and sank to his knees.

Charlie grabbed Bond by the hair and jerked him upright, turning the hapless prisoner around to face him. "Now let me explain something to you, Mr. Pascal Bond," Charlie said.

"And we want you to listen real good," Gideon said.

"You got us in an awful fix," Charlie went on. "Our lives is in danger from the Texas Rangers and ever' other lawman in this state. We was pursuing an honorable intention of ridding the world of a gang o' outlaws and thieving murderers on a mission that you give us. Do you foller me, Mr. Pascal Bond?"

Bond, rubbing his sore cheek, nodded. "Yes."

"But you was setting us up to fail, wasn't you?" Guy asked.

Charlie added, "Worser than that, Mr. Pascal Bond, you was setting us up to get killed. That's what you was doing."

Bond wisely kept silent.

"You may think it's terrible unfair for three of us to be on you all at once like this. It might look like we're cowards and bullies, but right now we got no choice," Charlie said. "You forced our hand in the baddest possible way, Mr. Pascal Bond."

"Now, as you prob'ly figgered out from the way we're acting and talking, the three of us are desperate men," Guy said. "And we ain't got a hell of a lot to lose right now."

Gideon poked Bond. "Which puts you in a bad way."

"And that's only fair," Guy emphasized.

"That's right," Charlie said. "I'm gonna ask you some questions. If we don't like the answers you give, them punches we just thumped you with is gonna seem like love taps."

Bond snuffed and rubbed his nose. "I won't lie to you. I realize I'm completely at your mercy."

"Now you're being sensible," Gideon said.

"The first question is, who is Ace Erickson running his organization with there in Stavanger?" Charlie asked. "Is it just with Gustavo Fairweather or is some sharper involved along with 'em?"

"Gustavo Fairweather is helping Ace Erickson, of course, but there is also a lawyer by the name of Maxwell Banter," Bond answered. "Banter makes all the arrangements for bribes. Naturally, it takes Gustavo Fairweather to run the gang."

"And who're their contacts in the state government?" Charlie wanted to know.

"A judge in Fort Worth by the name of Bacon," Bond replied. "And me. I work inside the government for information, and Judge Bacon issues whatever legal papers and writs we need."

"That's all?" Guy asked incredulously. "Just two fellers?"

"Of course," Bond said. "We couldn't bring more people in on this. If we did so, it would only be a matter of time before something went wrong."

"Then how do you know what the railroad is doing?" Gideon inquired.

"We have a telegrapher in Mineral Wells," Bond said. "He works in the central office there where information on all rail shipments are sent through. If one looks good, he tells us. The judge sends a messenger with the information to Ace Erickson or Maxwell Banter in Stavanger."

"Now ain't that slick?" Guy remarked.

"And what's ol' Gustavo Fairweather up to these days?" Charlie asked.

"He was supposed to build the gang back up. He's managed to hire on six more pistoleros."

"Are they still at T. J. Grogan's ranch?" Gideon asked.

Bond shook his head. "They don't figure it's safe there anymore. They're holed up at a line camp in Cooke County."

"Sit down, Mr. Pascal Bond," Charlie said. He waited for the man to slump to the ground. He motioned Guy and Gideon to follow him off a few paces. "We got two things to do," he whispered.

"Let's do 'em," Guy said. "What are they?"

"We got to get them warrants on us canceled," Charlie said. "And we got to get Gustavo Fairweather and that gang out o' Cooke County and into a showdown."

Gideon rubbed his whiskery chin. "Any particular way you want us to accomplish them things?"

"First thing we do is visit this Judge Bacon in Fort Worth," Charlie said. "It ain't far away. We'll have Pascal Bond tell him to get them warrants killed off quick."

"What makes you think the judge is gonna do that?" Guy asked.

"The fact that we'll be there and Bond will be there is gonna convince him that the end is near," Charlie said. "He'll get that paper off our backs and probably skedaddle for safer grounds."

"That makes sense," Gideon mused.

"Then what're we gonna do?" Guy requested to know.

"We'll visit that telegrapher and have him send out official telegrams to the law telling 'em that the warrants on us three is now null and void," Charlie said. "But not before having the judge send his messenger to Ace Erickson about a shipment of gold on a train going through Denton County."

Gideon laughed. "Damn! Ace Erickson won't be able to resist that."

"Neither will Gustavo Fairweather," Guy said. "And I presume instead o' gold, there'll be us three in that baggage car like y'all done that time between Longview and Marshall."

"This'll be the third job we been laying for 'em," Gideon said. "Which goes to prove that greed is pure bad for some folks, ain't it?"

"That's right," Charlie said.

Guy grinned. "At least this time I won't have to worry about you two shooting me."

"Nope," Gideon agreed. "But there'll be Gustavo Fairweather and six hardcases to do the job."

"Let's get rolling," Charlie said. He led the others back to Bond. He pulled the crook to his feet. "We're gonna make a call on Judge Bacon. You know where he lives in Fort Worth, don't you?"

"Yes," Bond answered.

"Then let's go see the man," Guy said.

Bond reluctantly mounted up with the others and pointed in the direction they were to go. He rode dejected, knowing that everything he had worked for in the scheme with Ace Erickson was starting to unravel. All he could hope for was fo the three Rangers' luck to turn sour. And he con soled himself with the thought they'd had mor bad fortune than good lately. If that trend contin ued, things could still work out for him.

It took almost an hour of steady riding in th dark to reach the judge's residence in Fort Worth After dismounting and tying up their horses at th hitching rail by a picket fence, the group of mer went up on the porch and banged on the door.

"Call him," Charlie hissed at Bond.

"Judge Bacon!" Bond yelled out. "It's me, Pas cal Bond."

Guy punched him. "Keep it up. We ain't got al night."

Bond took a deep breath. "Judge Bacon! Judge Bacon! It's me, Pascal Bond! Judge Bacon!"

A window opened on the second floor. "What're you doing out there this time of night, Bond?"

"Important business, Your Honor," Bond said. "I've got to see you."

"Tell him it has to do with Ace Erickson," Charlie commanded.

"It has to do with Ace Erickson," Bond dutifully reported.

"Shhh! Don't say that name too loud," Judge Bacon admonished him. "I'll be right down." The window slammed shut.

"You let me do the talking," Charlie told Bond. "You just follow my lead, savvy?"

"I understand," Bond said.

Moments later the judge appeared at the door. He was surprised to see the three men with Bond. "Now what's going on?" he asked.

"You got legal papers and forms here?" Charlie asked.

"Sure I do," the judge replied. "I do work at home in the evenings so's I don't have to stay late at the courthouse. Why?"

"On account o' you're gonna lift three warrants pronto," Charlie Delano said. "Let's get inside and behave ourselves."

"Do as he says, Your Honor," Bond urged him.

"Of course," the judge said, sensing something was terribly wrong. He led them into his house and back to his study. He lit a lantern, then looked at the four men. "What did you say you wanted me to do?"

"You're gonna write out papers canceling the warrants on Charlie Delano, Guy Tyrone, and Gideon Magee," Charlie told him.

"But we just—" The judge began to sweat. "Am I to presume that you three are messieurs Delano, Tyrone, and Magee?"

"That's about the size of it, Judge," Charlie said.

"Now listen," Bacon said. "I didn't know what this was all about. I just issued warrants like I was instructed. That's all."

"Don't say any more than you have to," Bond advised the judge. "Just do as they tell you."

"Oh, God, Bond! I knew this wouldn't work out!" the judge whined.

"Kill them warrants!" Charlie exclaimed.

"It won't take long," the judge assured them. He sat down at his desk and pulled out some legal forms from the middle drawer. After dipping his pen in the inkwell, he began to write.

"Where's your messenger?" Charlie asked.

The judge looked up. "That'd be my clerk. He has a room at the back of the house."

Charlie nudged Guy. "Go fetch the son of a bitch."

"You bet," Guy said. He hurried off to tend to the chore.

The judge continued working, sweat beading on his forehead in spite of the coolness of the room. He stopped finally and looked up at Charlie. "It's completed, sir." He got the embosser bearing his official seal and stamped each paper with it. "That proves it is authentic," he explained, trying to be helpful.

Charlie, familiar with legal documents through years of working with them as a lawman, carefully scrutinized the papers. "Good. As of now we're all three reinstated in the Texas Rangers, by God!"

Guy appeared with a hastily dressed, very sleepy, and confused young man. Here's the messenger. He says his name is Jack."

"Howdy, Jack," Charlie said. "The judge has an errand for you."

Jack looked at the judge. "What do you want me to do?"

Judge Bacon jerked a thumb in Charlie Delano's direction. "Ask him."

"That's right. I'm the man that knows all the right things to do," Charlie said. "You go to Stavanger and tell Ace Erickson that tomorrow morning's 9:05 northbound Texas Central out of Dallas has a shipment of gold dollars."

"Yes, sir," Jack said, not really knowing what was going on. "How big a shipment?"

"Oh, let's see," Charlie said, thinking. He looked at Guy. "How big a shipment there, Guy?"

"Oh, fifty thousand dollars' worth," Guy said.

"Got it, Jack?" Charlie asked.

"Yes, sir."

"Then get moving," Charlie urged him.

Jack uttered a curt good-bye, then, knowing the message was one of great importance, rushed out of the room.

Charlie turned his attention to Pascal Bond and Judge Bacon. "Right now we ain't got a lot of time to spend on you two," he said. "That means you got a couple of choices. You can stay here and get arrested in the next coupla days or you can get the hell out o' Texas. Either way suits me."

"Me too," Gideon Magee said. "On account o' when this thing is over I'm going back to being a federal marshal and I'll hunt you both down no matter where you go to hide in the U.S. of A." He chuckled. "You might consider Canada. The climate's a mite cool, but you can stay there out o' trouble."

Bacon bowed his head. "Oh, God!" he moaned.

Pascal Bond, his face a mask of despair, sat down in a nearby chair. "Your Honor," he said to his partner in crime. "What if we turn state's evidence?"

"Don't be stupid!" Bacon hissed at him.

"Adios, you two," Charlie said. "C'mon, boys, we got to go see a telegrapher and get his name while he sends out the official word over the wire about our warrants being killed off. Then it's off to Dallas for a train ride to meet with Gustavo Fairweather and the Ace Erickson gang."

Pascal Bond felt a surge of defiant anger well up. "If Gustavo wipes you three off the face of the earth, our troubles will be over."

Guy laughed. "So will ours."

"Don't make fun," Gideon cautioned his younger friend. "It could happen."

Nineteen

Charlie Delano, as usual, was in the lead as he and his two Ranger companions strode noisily across the wooden expanse of the Dallas train depot loading dock. Their spurs jangled in time to the clomp of their heavy boots on the structure. The noise seemed to emphasize their eager impatience to get on with the dangerous job they faced.

The trio had loaded their horses in an empty cattle car moments before, and now were headed for the vehicle they would ride in. Going directly up to the baggage car of the northbound 9:05 of the Texas Central Railroad, Charlie banged on the door with his fist.

"Open up!" he bellowed.

"Says who?" came a question by a muffled voice inside.

"The Texas By God Rangers, that's who!" Charlie yelled. "Open up, I say! In the name of the law. In the name of Texas. And in the name of Cap'n Charlie Delano."

The door slid open and a railroad clerk looked down at the three Rangers. "Howdy."

"Howdy," Charlie said. He showed his badge. "We'll be riding with you." He hopped up onto the car and swung himself inside. "I'm the Cap'n Charlie Delano I mentioned before."

"I kinda figgered you was," the other man said. "I'm the chief clerk on this crew."

"Hurry up, boys," Charlie said to Guy Tyrone and Gideon Magee behind him.

After Guy and Gideon were aboard, the chief clerk slammed the door shut. He was curious as to what interest the three Rangers would have in taking that particular train. "What can we do for you?" he asked.

"You're gonna be hit today," Charlie informed him. "By a gang o' train and bank robbers."

"Are you loco?" the railroad man asked. "We ain't carrying nothing worth getting robbed for."

"Maybe not," Guy chimed in. "But them bandits think so. And that's what counts."

"Does the engineer know?" the chief clerk asked.

"Nope," Charlie answered.

"We don't want to cause him no unnecessary worry," Gideon added. "And neither do you, right?"

"I reckon not," the chief clerk said. He checked his watch. "Anyhow, we'll be pulling out o' Dallas here in another five minutes."

"Well, you boys get on with your mail sorting and other duties," Charlie said. "Me and my Rangers is just gonna make ourselves comfortable 'til the shooting starts."

The chief clerk looked straight into Charlie's face. "Let me tell you something, Cap'n. I'll fight like hell to protect a shipment my company has took responsibility for, but I ain't about to get my ass shot over whatever is going on today. Savvy?"

"Sure. When the gunplay starts, you and them other railroad men can take cover behind them trunks and boxes back there," Charlie said. "That'd be right sensible of you."

"We're sensible fellers," one of the other clerks said. "You'll see that when bullets commence to fly around here."

By the time Charlie, Guy, and Gideon settled down on the floor in the far end of the car, the train whistle sounded from the engine.

They could hear the conductor calling out as he walked along the platform. "All aboard! All aboard!"

Moments later, the train began to move. It took off slowly, at about the speed of a walking man, but gradually the speed increased until the iron wheels clicked against the joint bars in an ever-increasing staccato.

"We're on our way!" Guy called out over the noise.

"Where do you reckon they'll hit us?" Gideon wondered.

Charlie looked at Guy. "You learned some about ol' Gustavo Fairweather," he said. "Where do you think he'll stop the train?"

"Well, let's see," Guy mused. "I reckon we can expect trouble between Denton and Sanger."

"I don't know," Gideon said. "That's pretty close to Stavanger, ain't it?"

"Yeah," Guy agreed. "But they're staying at that line camp in Cooke County. They'll be figuring to run up there to settle in while Gustavo doubles back to take the loot to Ace Erickson."

"That makes sense," Charlie said. He got up and walked over to the chief clerk. "What time will we be running past Denton?"

"Well, we'll stop there at about nine-forty," the railroad man answered. "It won't take more'n five or ten minutes to load on whatever baggage and passengers they is there. So we should be rolling out o' Denton at about nine-forty-five or ten minutes afore ten."

"Much obliged," Charlie said. He went back to the two Rangers and sat down. "Sometime shortly after ten o'clock, we're gonna be in a gunfight, boys."

"Good," Guy said, looking at his watch. "That gives me time for a quick nap."

"You could sleep through a damn tornado," Gideon Magee remarked with a touch of admiration in his voice.

But Guy didn't hear. He'd already leaned back and drifted off as he unconsciously rocked with the rhythm of the swaying train. His slumber was light enough that he would know if anything happened, yet deep enough that he snored softly, the sound unheard over the noise of the moving train.

They arrived in Denton on time, coming to a jerky, clamorous stop that shook the car as its momentum continued against the engine's brakes. It was noisy and bumpy, but not enough to wake up Guy Tyrone, who still snoozed away.

The stay in Denton was only seven minutes. More calls of "All aboard!" from the conductor heralded the resumption of the journey. Charlie looked at his watch, then at Gideon.

Gideon grinned and pointed to Guy. "Still napping away.

"That boy has ice water in his veins," Charlie said.

"And solid wood in his head," Gideon added.

"I heard that," Guy said. Then he went back to sleep.

The train rolled on for another eight minutes. When it was exactly ten o'clock, Charlie stood up. "Let's get ready." He nudged Guy with his boot.

Guy came wide awake in an instant. He stood up and checked his carbine. A quick pump of the cocking lever chambered a round. "Bring 'em on," he said.

Charlie and Gideon also readied their long guns for the fight. Gideon went to the door and peered through the crack. "Suppose they don't show up?"

Guy laughed. "They'll show up. You talk that much gold to Ace Erickson and Gustavo Fairweather, and they're gonna be there with bells on. At least Gustavo will."

Before any more remarks could be made, the train began a lurching motion of slowing down. The movement was so violent that the men in the car almost lost their balance.

"That's them!" Guy yelled. "They've prob'ly got logs on the track."

Charlie signaled to the railroad men. "Take cover!"

The train came to the end of its abrupt stopping motion. Some yells outside could be heard, then the sound of boots running across the railbed toward the car.

"Get ready!" Guy said.

A pounding on the door punctuated his warning. "Open up or we'll dynamite the damn car!"

Charlie yelled back, "Hang on. Don't use no explosives, please! I'll open her for you." He worked the hasp, then glanced back at Guy and Gideon. Ready?"

They both nodded, their lips pursed in anticipation for the hell about to break loose. "Go on!" Gideon said anxiously.

Charlie pulled the door open, keeping himself behind it. Both Guy and Gideon fired quick shots at the bandits outside.

Two of the robbers momentarily wobbled under the blow of the slugs, before toppling to the ground. A couple more of the gang, game and angry at this violent surprise, returned fire.

Charlie now joined the battle. Two well-aimed bullets found their marks, eliminating the attack at the baggage car's side. "Let's go!"

The three Rangers charged out the door, leaping to the ground and rolling. They came up on their knees, the three carbines spitting hot lead at the startled gang.

One of the bandits yelled out, "Oh, shit! Not again!"

Guy recognized him as Lee Fenney. Only a few feet from him, Elmer Sherman took a shot in the belly. He doubled over and went down, rolling around to a sitting position. That netted him a second bullet. This one smacked straight into his head, blowing his life away.

Fenney tried to fight back, but simultaneous hits lifted him from his feet and deposited him on his butt. He dropped his six-gun, then held up his hands to surrender. It was too late. At this last gesture he died, toppling over. Another bandit's career ended.

Up by the engine, Gustavo Fairweather watched in rage as his planned robbery unraveled before his eyes. He recognized Guy Tyrone when the Ranger leaped from the baggage car. A quickly aimed shot at the former gang member missed, and Fairweather decided he didn't have the time to chance another. He spun toward the engineer and fireman. "If nobody else pays for this, you two will!" he hissed. He deliberately shot the unarmed men, putting the bullets into their heads. Then, scrambling over the fresh corpses, he rushed down from the locomotive and ran for the trees near the railroad tracks where the gang's horses were tied up.

He wasted no time getting his mount and swinging up into the saddle. With a shout and a curse, he galloped out the other side of the copse and turned toward Stavanger.

The last of the gang went down under the three Rangers' fusillades of carbine shots as Fairweather rode wildly to escape the scene of death.

Twenty

Driven by raw fear, Gustavo Fairweather rode hard, fast, and reckless. He cussed and slapped his horse with vicious swipes of the reins as he pounded across the hard Texas ground toward Stavanger.

Fairweather was a professional outlaw, lawman, and gunfighter who had worked those three crossover crafts for sixteen years. The fact that he had survived that much time, taking only two bullets into his hide—a shoulder hit during a cattle-rustling episode in the Indian Territory and a slug that gouged out a large hunk of his thigh during a grudge fight in Galveston—was testimony to his skill with a gun.

But there was another reason for his success too. Gustavo Fairweather had an uncanny sense of judgment that led him into good situations and out of bad predicaments. It was this instinct that led him to get tied up with Ace Erickson's operation in the first place.

Now that same ability to figure out situations had now driven him to the decision that it was high time to get the hell out of there.

The only reason he was headed for Stavanger was because he had some money coming, and he was damn well going to get it. If it weren't for that, he would have been galloping toward the refuge of west Texas at that particular moment.

Fairweather glanced back to see if he was being pursued. When he noted the clear landscape behind him, he was a bit surprised. He'd expected the three Rangers to be right on his heels as he made his break from the locomotive. Especially after shooting down the engineer and fireman in cold blood. But a few sporadic moments of resistance by the last survivors of the gang had evidently slowed them down enough to give him a chance for a clean, albeit, fast ride to Ace Erickson to get a final payoff.

Growing nervousness and fear built up a desperate anger in the fleeing man. He cruelly dug his spurs into the horse and yelled out in a hoarse, raging voice.

"Go on, damn you! Run! Run, you son of a bitch!"

Man and animal skirted a thicket, then swung back on a direct route back to their destination. Foamy perspiration began oozing from the horse's hide and his tongue now hung out, streaming a long, thick string of saliva. Fairweather noticed, but had no concern for his mount's physical condition.

"Gallop! You lop-eared bastard! Damn your butt! I'll run you 'til you drop dead!"

A bit more than a half hour of hard riding finally brought the sight of Stavanger on the horizon. The horse seemed to sense getting there meant the end of its torment. Taking equine courage, it stretched its stride and picked up speed. Fairweather took another look to the rear. Satisfied he was not being pursued, he settled in for the final distance into town.

The sound of the hoofbeats changed as the terrain went from open prairie to the hardpacked dirt of Stavanger's main street. When he reached the Ace of Diamonds Saloon, Fairweather brutally pulled on the reins and ended the run.

The man leaped from the saddle and rushed across the boardwalk, charging into the bar. The bartender, surprised at the sudden, blustery appearance, looked up. "What tarnation's going on, Gustavo?"

"Where the hell is Ace?" Fairweather demanded to know.

"In the back room with Banter and Dinah," the man answered.

Fairweather went across the room and pushed the door open. "It's over!" he announced.

Ace Erickson, Dinah Walters, and Maxwell Banter were as startled by his unexpected entrance as the bartender had been.

Ace asked, "What's over, Gustavo?"

"The whole operation," Fairweather answered. "That train robbery went to hell when them three Rangers—" He glared at Maxwell Banter. "—the three you had warrants set up for—was waiting for us in the baggage car. They shot us up bad. Just like they done twice before. I'm the only one to get away."

Banter shook his head in dismay. "What the hell are you talking about?"

"Just what I said!" Fairweather shouted. "They ain't wanted by the law no more. That's obvious to even the densest son of a bitch! They got their badges back, so they're back on the prod. Whoever was helping us out has give in. We ain't got no more protection."

"They must have gotten to Judge Bacon," Maxwell Banter said.

Ace Erickson nodded. "Yeah. And Pascal Bond too."

Dinah Walter was puzzled. "What does all that mean?"

"Just what I said," Fairweather said. "The law is gonna be all over us now. We can't pay or bribe our way out of trouble no more." He pointed a finger at Ace. "And I want a big hunk o' cash to get me to friendlier country."

"That's something we can all use," Ace said. "I always expected this day. The safe up in my room has three big packets of money. One for each of us."

The woman was furious. "What about me? You can't just go off and leave me!"

"You want to bet, my love?" Ace said. "You have no worries anyhow. You're a complete unknown in this scheme. So relax." He started for the door, gesturing to Fairweather and Banter. "Come on!" He left the office with his companions in crime behind him. "Get to the livery stables and saddle two horses," he ordered the bartender as the three crossed the room.

"Three," Fairweather corrected. "Mine is blowed out from the ride back here."

"I'm on my way, Mr. Erickson," the bartender said.

Ace charged up the stairs two steps at a time. He went to his apartment, allowing the others to follow him in. A small safe sat off to one side of the dresser. Dinah joined the group as Ace began working the dial.

Dinah tugged at Fairweather's sleeve. "Was Guy Tyrone with the other two?"

"Yeah," Fairweather answered. "Alive and well and shooting like a crazy man. If you want to know how he is, just stick around. He'll be showing up directly."

"Maybe I'll do that," Dinah said. She looked at Ace. "Maybe I'll just do that."

Fairweather snorted. "I kinda figgered you'd got sweet on him."

"I don't care what you figured," Dinah said. She quickly left the room.

Ace, completely unconcerned about Dinah's feelings, opened the door of the safe and reached inside. "Hold on, boys. The money is in the back." He felt around for a few moments. "Here it is."

"About time," Banter complained.

Ace pulled himself out of the interior of the safe, then suddenly spun on his heel. A pistol in his hand spit fire, the two slugs striking Banter.

Gustavo Fairweather had drawn his own Colt moments before. This wasn't the first time he'd known of a crime boss to lose out, and he expected the worst sort of treachery. He pumped three shots into Ace Erickson, who was slammed back into the safe. He bounced forward on his knees, then went straight down on his face.

Maxwell Banter staggered over to the sofa and sat down, bleeding heavily. He was rapidly going into shock. He stared at Ace's body, taking little note when Fairweather rolled the corpse aside to loot the safe.

"Oh, God," Banter wheezed. He sat back and stared up at the ceiling, then died.

Gustavo Fairweather found a large canvas sack filled with twenty-dollar gold pieces. It was heavy as hell, but he was a strong man. He walked to the door and out on the landing. As he started for the stairs, he heard a noise downstairs. Easing over to the rail he looked down into the barroom.

Charlie Delano, Guy Tyrone, and Gideon Magee had entered the saloon. Formed in loose skirmish line, the three Rangers moved cautiously across the room toward the office door.

Fairweather grinned to himself. It would be easy. Three quick shots. And at the range he barely had to aim. Killing the lawmen would take no more than just pointing the six-shooter downstairs. He picked out Guy Tyrone as the first target, aligning his sights on the Ranger. He began the pull on the trigger, still grinning.

The shot blasted out.

Charlie, Guy, and Gideon's eyes turned upward in time to see the derringer bullet hit Fairweather in the side of the chest. The shock of the slug's strike pushed the outlaw back from the railing. Groaning heavily, he stepped forward and crashed through the flimsy wooden barrier, splintering it.

Fairweather fell to the barroom, crashing heavily to the floor. The moneybag with him broke open, sending out a shower of large, gold coins.

The three Rangers glanced over to the other side of the landing. They saw Dinah Walters holding the small, smoking pistol in her hand. She smiled at Guy. "That's one you owe me," she said in a sultry voice.

"I reckon I do," Guy said. "Where do we find Ace Erickson and Maxwell Banter?"

"They're in Ace's office," Dinah answered. "Both dead."

Charlie tipped his hat in a polite manner. "Am I to presume that they was did in by Gustavo Fairweather? Or maybe you done the honors, ma'am."

"Gustavo sent them to their just rewards," Dinah said. She hadn't taken her eyes off Guy. "How have you been? I haven't seen you for a while."

"Oh, quite tolerable, Miss Dinah," Guy said. "These fellers here is Cap'n Charlie Delano and Ranger Gideon Magee."

"At your service, ma'am," Gideon said.

"It's a pleasure, ma'am," Charlie said.

The atmosphere of relief gave way to the sudden sound of arriving horses outside. The trio started to take cover when the loud voice of Ranger Captain Pete Dawson could be heard.

"Charlie Delano! Are you in there?"

"Sure," Charlie yelled back. "But don't come in shooting, Pete. I had them warrants on us took away."

"I know," Dawson said. He entered the saloon with two more Rangers behind him. "When I heard, I was plumb glad, Charlie. And I figgered I'd find you right here in Stavanger."

"We wrapped her up all right," Charlie said. "You didn't seem to have no trouble knowing where we'd be."

"I been trailing after you," Pete admitted. "You boys left a passel o' dead Mexicans down there in Dallas. If I was you, I wouldn't go back to that barrio for a spell if ever."

"That's good advice," Charlie said.

"At least you got some money coming out o' the deal," Pete said. "One of 'em was a wanted man by the name o' Memo Chavito."

"That'll make up for the money we lost," Charlie said.

Guy looked at him wide-eyed. "What money is that?"

"We don't get paid for the time we was under warrant," Charlie explained.

"That's right," Gideon said.

"But it was all a put-up," Guy protested.

"It don't matter," Charlie said with a shrug of his shoulders. "We was still legally not in the Rangers at the time. So we wasn't on the payroll."

"Then I'm glad I got that reward money," Guy said. He brightened. "Along with what I got in them robberies."

Captain Pete Dawson looked at him. "What robberies?"

"Never mind, I was just jawing," Guy said. He

glared at Charlie and Gideon. "Like I told you two galoots, this is the absolute last time I'm working for a big organization. From now on I'm going back to being a small-town deputy." He took off his Ranger badge and tossed it to Charlie. "I quit."

"You leaving town pretty quick?" Gideon asked.

Guy glanced up at Dinah. "Oh, maybe I'll stick around a little longer." He waved at her. "How about a drink with me, Miss Dinah?"

Gideon growled. "He'd find a perty woman in a scrub desert!" He unpinned his Ranger badge and handed it over to Charlie. "I reckon I'm heading back for Judge Parker's court. Being a U.S. deputy marshal is more my style."

Charlie shrugged. "This is gonna break up a mighty good team. I'm sorry to see you go. But I'll make you look good in my report when I write it up."

Pete Dawson pulled a document from his vest pocket. "Charlie, this here is orders for you. Seems we got a ruckus over cattle rustling down there near Progreso."

"Yeah?" Charlie asked. "I'll bet it's *bandidos* coming across the border. That'll be a tough case." He looked for Gideon, but he was already out the door and mounting up. A glance at Guy showed him in deep, intimate conversation with Dinah Walters. Charlie laughed. "It looks like I'll be going this one alone."

"Looks like it," Pete Dawson said. "C'mon. I'll ride with you to Dallas. You can turn in your report before you head out on the new case."

"Sure. I also got to get warrants out on Pascal Bond and Judge Bacon," Charlie said, stepping over Gustavo Fairweather's body. "So long, Guy. You're a mighty good pard, by God!"

But Guy didn't hear a word he said.

Epilogue

Guy Tyrone's chair was tipped back with his feet up on his desk. He'd managed to retrieve his billy club made of jirara wood, but things had been so quiet, it was kept in the ammunition drawer under the gunrack.

As the new sheriff in town, he'd been spending the first three days of his job getting acquainted with the people and places of this fresh area of responsibility. Now, with those preliminaries over, he allowed himself to settle into a quiet routine that he knew would be broken now and then by some disturbance.

He drifted off into a brief nap, but the sounds of a squeaky wheel on a wagon rolling past brought him back to wakefulness. Irritated, he stood up and went outside on the boardwalk.

"Howdy, Sheriff," a citizen said, hurrying past. "How's the new job?"

"Tolerable," Guy said with a friendly nod.

The man stopped and turned around.. "Stavanger is gonna be a nice town now that Ace Erickson and Gustavo Fairweather are gone."

"I'll see that it is," Guy said. "That's what I took the job for."

"And you've been doing fine," the citizen said.

"I hear you broke up a fight last night down by the livery stable. And even throwed them brawlers in the calaboose."

"That I did," Guy said. "And they're still in them cells cooling their heels."

"Yep. You're doing a fine job." The man waved and went on his way.

"Nice to be appreciated," Guy said to himself. He turned and strolled down the street in the opposite direction. Walking slowly, he returned the friendly greetings given him until he reached the Ace of Diamonds Saloon. He went inside and nodded to the barkeep. "Is the boss in?"

"Back in the office, Sheriff," the man replied.

Guy walked over to the door and rapped on it. He entered the room and grinned. "Howdy, Dinah."

"Hello, Guy," Dinah Walters said, looking up from her bookkeeping. "Or should I address you as Sheriff?"

He went to her side, bending over and kissing the woman on the cheek. She lifted her face and Guy pressed his lips against hers. "Why don't you just call me darling?"

"All right, darling," Dinah said.

Guy pointed to the figures she was working on. "Is ever'thing shaping up all right?"

"There wasn't a lot left of the business after the auditors from the state government got done," Dinah said. "But there's enough for a decent start."

"You'll make a go of it," Guy said.

"When we're married, this'll all be yours," Dinah said. "Are you going to let me make you into a gentleman saloonkeeper, or are you going to keep that sheriff's job?"

"I might," Guy said. "To tell you the truth, honey, I'm gonna have to give the idea of running a saloon a lot of thought. I don't know nothing about it."

"I can teach you," Dinah said. "Don't worry."

A knock on the door interrupted them. The railroad telegrapher at the town depot came inside with an envelope. "This just came for you, Sheriff Tyrone. It looked important, so I didn't want to leave it at your office." He chuckled. "I knew where to find you if'n you wasn't down to the jail."

Guy grinned. "Thanks, Tom." He took the message and opened it. "Oh, goddamn it!"

"What's the matter?" Dinah asked in alarm.

"It's from Charlie Delano down there in Progreso," he said. "He's working on a rustling case."

"So why is he sending you a telegram?" Dinah asked suspiciously.

Guy took a deep breath. "Well—"

"Well, what?" Dinah snapped.

"It looks like Charlie needs a little help," Guy said. "It seems most of the trouble is coming from south of the border. That makes it double difficult for him."

"So why is Charlie Delano telling you all this?" Dinah wanted to know. Her voice had a nervous edge to it.

"He kind o' wonders if I'd mind another short stint in the Texas Rangers," Guy explained.

"You just tell him no!" Dinah said. "Tell him absolutely not!"

"Well, Dinah, it ain't that easy," Guy said.

"I knew this would happen," Dinah said sadly.

Charlie didn't say anything more. He nodded an absentminded good-bye, and quickly left the saloon and returned to his office. He sat down at the desk and took off the sheriff's badge, putting it down in front of him. Taking a piece of paper, pen, and ink bottle from the drawer, he began to write out his resignation as the sheriff of Stavanger, Texas. When he finished, he went to the gunrack for his carbine and walked out on the boardwalk.

Dinah walked into the office, stopping by the door. "When are you coming back?"

"I'm afraid working for Cap'n Charlie Delano is gonna be a permanent part o' my life, darling," Guy said. "I don't think I'll be coming back."

"I won't be married to some wandering Ranger," Dinah said angrily. "I won't wait for you, Guy Tyrone."

"I didn't figger you would," Guy said. "But it's something I got to do. If you won't have it that way, it just ain't meant to be."

"Good-bye," Dinah said. "And to tell you the truth, I'm not surprised."

"I reckon I'm not either," Guy said. He grinned wryly. "It looks pretty certain that I'm gonna end up a lonely ol' bachelor Ranger cap'n like Charlie."

"I don't give a damn how you end up," Dinah said. She calmed down. "I didn't mean that. I'm sorry. You'll always be somebody special to me, Guy."

"That's the way I feel about you, Dinah," Guy

said. "So long and good luck."

Dinah made no reply. She quickly turned and walked back to the saloon in slow, sad steps.

Guy watched her for a couple of moments, then went on down the street toward the livery stable.

"I wonder if I'll reach Charlie Delano before Gideon Magee does," he mused to himself.